Ms.Lloby do you know how much of a blessing you are? Do you know how much your anointing will manifest? You are simply amazing and I just think that God can't He can't. God bless you. —Olivia

All Over Again…For Real THIS Time

By: Olivia N. Williams

Table of Contents

Chapter 1: Crossing Paths...3

Chapter 2: A Very Good Start..17

Chapter 3: A Sharp Left Turn...28

Chapter 4: All Over Again..37

Chapter 5: For Real THIS Time..47

Chapter 6: Divine Epiphany...54

Chapter 7: Speak on it, James...96

Chapter 8: The Storm..112

Chapter 9: Eternal Happiness...136

Chapter 1: Crossing Paths

Every day, on the way to my truck, I walk past that old, raggedy crack house...I remember a time when that old house was the abode to a very nice family; all it took was that one shooting down the street. That nice white house with those classy black shutters, and the simplistically elegant front porch with those not too steep stairs and beautiful, dark, green grass was abandoned and too expensive for that neighborhood to be sold, so nobody ever bought it. After the realtors gave up hope of selling the house, a man finagled his way in and the degeneration began. That house went from beautiful abode, to the crack house up the street. That crack house became the talk of the town after while. Every time I pass by that old, raggedy crack house, I see James at his regular spot, on that jagged rock right near the steps of that old, raggedy crack house. James and I have the same conversation every day, but there was something different about today...

***

"Now baby, I know you're not gonna pass me by without speakin'," says James with that full, snaggletooth grin he always had whenever he sees Lauryn.

"Hello, James," says Lauryn as she stops, turns around and chuckles and looks to her old friend.

"When we goin' out, girl?"

"Whenever you get a job."

"Hm! I got a job! A good job, too!"

"James, I pass by this place every single day and I see you. You can't be at work if you're here all day, baby."

"It's a night job."

"Oh, really, you must go to work after I leave every night huh?"

"That's right; I gotta make sure none of these here folks mess with that beautiful Caddy."

Lauryn laughs heartily and James joins in the laugh. The others around them stared, mostly at them; others stared into places not of this earth.

"James, you need to be in church."

"Now you know I only like it when you preach, girl."

"Now *you* know I preach most every Sunday."

"So, if I come to church this Sunday, can I take you out to dinner Sunday evening?"

Lauryn gives off a façade as if she's seriously pondering the thought. "I'll think about it."

"That sounds good enough to me baby, I's keepin' hope alive!"

Lauryn takes a long, hard look into James's eyes, she notices something different about him today; he was giving off a different vibe.

Something in my spirit ain't right, there's something different about him. I need to have a talk with him.

"Come here James, I need to talk to you for a minute."

James gets up and walks with Lauryn toward her vehicle and he can't help but to wonder what this talk is going to be about. They stop at the front of Lauryn's truck.

"James, how are you?"

"I'm makin' it."

"Are you high right now?"

"No."

Little did Lauryn know, James was in fact telling the truth, she didn't believe him though.

"Mmhmm."

"I'm serious, I'm tryna do right."

Lauryn looks further into James's weak eyes.

Lauryn answers very sarcastically, "Are you?"

"I'm tired of this life, Lauryn. I want to do better."

"You promise to come to church with me, and I'll help you get help. Matter of fact, come on, let's go."

They proceed to get in the truck.

"Are you hungry, James?"

"I haven't eaten in about a week…"

"What would you like to eat?"

"Whatever you feed me."

"Well, we don't wanna upset your stomach, so we won't get anything too greasy. How about our old favorite place?"

"Whatever's clever darlin'."

After Lauryn starts her vehicle and is about to switch the gearshift, James grabs her hand and squeezes tightly. Lauryn looks at him with the most sincere gaze.

"You really are serious about this, James."

"Yes, I am," James says as he starts to sob.

"Let's get you something to eat."

There is a pause of great silence; Lauryn ponders how she's going to help her old friend out, and James wonders how somebody could care for him so greatly after all he's been through and all he's done.

"I hope this means you're coming to church with me on Sunday, James."

"Yes ma'am."

"If you can promise me that you will stay put, I'll let you sleep on my couch until Sunday."

"Lauryn Nevaeh Jones, you truly are something else. God broke the mold when He made you girl."

At this point, Lauryn knows full well that James is sober; he used to say her full name like that all the time back in the day.

Lauryn chuckles, "You're quite the character yourself James Willard."

"I'm serious girl, you take care of me like no other. After everything went left, you were still there. I pushed everyone away, even you, and you were still around."

"Not one day of my life have I ever taken care of you. You're doing an…alright job taking care of yourself, there have just been times in the past when you've needed a little help."

"You remember back in college when I got really sick out of nowhere?"

"Of course I remember that, you were my only friend and I didn't have my partner in crime in class with me."

"I do remember something else though."

"Refresh my memory."

"I remember it like it was yesterday. It was junior year, right about the time of midterms, I sneezed and had a really bad nosebleed. You ran and got me some tissue and the bleeding just wouldn't stop, so you walked with me to the infirmary and you stayed with me. After the nurse finally got the bleeding to stop, I got really dizzy, so you walked with me to my apartment to make sure I made it back alright. The following morning you checked on me, I was feeling horrible and you said you had my back and would let all the professors know what was going on and that you would come over later and check on me. You told me that all the professors were concerned because they found out what happened and they all hoped I'd feel better soon. You got all my work for me that day and you came over. You said, 'you were quite the hot commodity today.' You smiled, you laughed, but as soon as you looked at me, you could tell I wasn't right. I remember you feeling my face for fever and I sho nuff had one, a pretty severe fever. You stayed with me overnight, and thank God you did. That was a rough night, I remember waking up suddenly unable to breathe and breaking out into a cold sweat. You wiped the sweat off my face, checked my fever periodically to watch it, and you comforted me. When I was by myself, I didn't think it was gonna end well for me, but my superwoman came to my rescue. You fed me, made sure I had everything I needed, kept me up to date with the academics, you stayed up all night to make sure I slept alright. There were times that I would be awake for a minute and I'd look at you and you were so stressed and so tired, but you never complained. After two weeks, I finally gained the strength to go to class and it was a struggle. You were there with me though, you walked with me to every class as you usually did, but you always had that look of concern in your eyes. Whenever we got back to my apartment, you'd make me rest when I wanted to get my work done. You were right every time though, when you made me rest was when I needed the rest the most. It took me over a month to get back to me, but you were there every step of the way, you were my backbone. You took care of me girl, don't deny it."

Lauryn had a distant stare as she listened to an event that she remembered as vividly as James did.

"I didn't take care of you, you weren't an invalid, you took care of yourself and I helped. I wasn't gonna do you like that, you were my best friend, I couldn't leave you hangin'."

By the time Lauryn finished with her argument, they arrived at what they knew as their favorite spot from back in the day, ordered to go and proceeded to Lauryn's apartment. As quickly as James could sit, that food was gone. Lauryn paced herself as she enjoyed a movie and James sat peacefully enjoying the movie himself. Sometimes, Lauryn would look over at James to see that same expression that he had earlier that day. There was definitely something bothering him, but Lauryn didn't want to push James into an unwanted conversation that could be just the trigger for him to cause harm to her or worse, himself. After the movie was over, Lauryn decided it was time to get some rest so she set up the couch nicely for James and James fell soundly asleep before his head completely hit the pillow.

It's Saturday, Saturday is Lauryn's day off, unfortunately a major case came in overnight and Lauryn had to be at work first thing in the morning. She left a note by James's pillow to let him know her whereabouts, a number she could be reached at, and breakfast was waiting for him when he was ready. After he woke up, he saw the note, ate his breakfast, and called her.

"Hello, beautiful."

"Good afternoon Mr. Willard, how'd you sleep?"

"Girl, I haven't had that good of a sleep since I don't know when."

"How are you?"

"I'm alright."

"How you feeling?"

"The most comfortable I've felt in ten years."

Lauryn paused as if she were shocked at his answer. Ten years ago was when they were last together, senior year of college.

I knew he was gonna say something like that, I don't know why I let it stun me though. "Well, I'm glad you still feel comfortable around me."

"You're only one who makes me feel comfortable."

Lauryn tries to shrug off that last statement as she moves subjects.

"I'll be here for a while, make yourself at home, I'll call you later on."

"Don't be gone too long, I already miss you too much."

They both laugh.

"Rest easy Mr. Willard."

"Work hard Ms. Jones."

"Bye."

"Bye."

About another four hours pass by before Lauryn gets a chance to even breathe so she's vacillating whether to call James or not. She also greatly ponders: what was on his mind last night, what made him want to change and be serious about it this time, is he still at the apartment, has he taken anything that he thinks is of value, has he gone to get his daily fix yet? These questions resonated with her, so she finally decided to call him just to see if he would answer.

I pray he's still there. If he's as sincere as I might think he is, he'll answer the phone with something slick to say with that silver tongue of his.

Lauryn proceeds to make the phone call.

"I missed you beautiful, I've been waiting to hear that voice."

"How's it going James? Have you been resting?"

"Yes ma'am, I went back to sleep shortly after I ate that wonderful breakfast you made."

"I gotta make sure you're eating, you gotta be attentive when you hear my sermon tomorrow. You *are* coming to church with me tomorrow right?"

"Yes ma'am."

"The good book does say come as you are, but we're going shopping today, I think you might feel better with a nice new suit on."

"Why do you treat me so well girl? I don't deserve it. I've done so much wrong in my life and you treat me so right."

"It's the right thing to do. Plus, once upon a time ago, you used to do a lot for me."

"Girl, I didn't do close to half of what you did for me."

"Your friendship meant a whole lot more than you think it did."

"Aw girl, don't start me to crying in here, you know I'm a sappy soul."

Lauryn laughs, "Well, I'll be home in a couple more hours, you think you can hold down the fort until I get there?"

"You know I got you. You ain't got to worry about nobody messin' with this place as long as there is breath in me."

"Alright now, that's what I like to hear."

"I can't wait till you return to me, I need my daily dose of that addictive smile."

"Quit playin' with me James," Lauryn said playfully. "I'll see you later."

"I'm counting the seconds."

The next couple of hours went by rather vastly and Lauryn returned home where James would be waiting for her with that same full, wide, snaggletooth grin that he has whenever he knows that he's getting ready to see her.

As soon as Lauryn caught a glimpse at James, she couldn't do anything but smile.

"Now I know you didn't miss me that much, James."

"You know I did."

Lauryn rolled her eyes, "How you doin'?"

"Fair to middlin', how are you doing beautiful?"

"I'm fine. You ready to go?"

"Yes ma'am."

"Alright, let's roll."

Lauryn and James spend a few hours out and about, she gets him a new suit for church service, a new pair of tennis shoes, and a couple items of casual clothes. All along, James had this puzzled look every time Lauryn would make a purchase for him. They get back to Lauryn's apartment, and she decided to let James sleep in the spare bedroom that night. This was the first time in about five years that James has even looked at a bed.

"I gotta tell you something, Law."

Oh Lord, what could possibly be wrong? He hasn't called me 'Law' in a long time, this has to be serious. "What's wrong?"

James takes a slow, deep breath and exhales even deeper and even slower. "This is hard to admit to you, Law."

When James found out that he and Lauryn were on the same path heading to law school after undergrad, he started calling her "Law" as a nickname, it was very befitting for her.

"Just tell me what's going on James, you're starting to worry me."

"Okay, here it is. Before it was time for you to get off work yesterday, I went and set up a fix that was far larger than what I usually get; I was going to overdose…but you saw something in me, you felt something wasn't right and you reached out to me…" James was seated at the edge of the bed and Lauryn was standing because she was preparing to leave the room; James grabbed both of Lauryn's hands and said with those same weak eyes that he had yesterday, "You saved my life. You stopped me from killing myself and I just want to thank you…*so*…much for that. I don't know what it was about yesterday, but you knew…you always know."

"It was God, James. My spirit felt very uneasy when I looked at you yesterday and God told me to go to you and talk to you. I didn't save your life, God did."

James broke out into a hysterical cry and leaned into Lauryn; Lauryn couldn't do anything but what she was used to doing, she comforted him.

After all the dust settled, Lauryn told James to get some rest for church in the morning. After leaving him and going into her room, the spirit moved Lauryn into a whole different direction for her morning sermon.

The next morning came, they got dressed, ate breakfast, and headed to church. On the ride to church, James decided to hold Lauryn's hand the whole way there and Lauryn did not object.

"When was the last time you heard me preach, James?"

"It's been at least two years."

"Well get ready, I've gained some more experience since then."

"Alright now! I'm ready for this!"

They get to the church, Lauryn seats James in a comfortable spot and leaves for her office in the back.

Lauryn preached what would be one of the strongest, most moving sermons that she had up to that point, and would be for a while. The whole entire church was set to fire and everybody was moved and crying and waving their arms up to God and running to the altar. She looks for James and sees him crying hysterically in his spot.

The service is over, each and every single person in attendance hugged Lauryn and thanked God Almighty for that sermon that was perfectly on time. The last person left and James is still sitting in that same spot.

"You alright James?" Lauryn was heavily concerned, he looked the same way he did when he was sick back in college.

"I'm ready."

"Ready for what?"

"I'm ready to end this life of blasphemy and live righteously for God. I'm ready to get right, Law."

"There is a rehab facility that is partnered with this church, I believe it is perfect for you. If you promise me that you will see this through this time, I will make sure that you get in, get taken care of properly, and that I see you as much as I can."

"I'm ready."

Chapter 2: A Very Good Start

If I must say so myself, James is off to a very good start. He's been going to his therapy sessions, he's keeping up with the doctor's appointments, he's attending my services regularly and he's even starting to look better. I'm so proud of him, he's actually seeing this thing through; he's for real THIS time.

***

"If I must say so myself, you're lookin' good Mr. Willard."

"I'm just trying to reach your level Ms. Jones."

Lauryn chuckles, "I'm decent, but I'm not extravagant."

"To me, you are the most beautiful girl in the world, you have no competition."

"You think you slick, you want something. What do you want?"

"You already know what I want. I want a date."

"Alright alright, I'll tickle your little fancy a bit. If you can get to a point where you can be released for a few hours here and there, we can go to lunch."

"THANK YA JESUS, SHE FINALLY SAID YES!!!!!!!!"

James was so excited for their upcoming "date," that was all he needed to keep him going. The next few months were great for James; he continued to go to his doctors' appointments, went to his therapy sessions and felt light as a feather.

This specific Sunday, Lauryn didn't preach, she was tired and wasn't exactly feeling her best, so she decided to go see her good friend to lift her spirits.

"You look a little down beautiful, something wrong?"

"I'm just a bit tired, I've been working really hard here lately; my clientele grew. I think all the exhaustion is just doing a number on my system, that's all. Nothing major."

"Aaaawwwww, my poor baby."

"I'll be alright; I just need a little rest."

"You know this is the same face you had back in the day whenever I caught those glimpses of you."

"Don't be too concerned, I'm going to sleep as soon as I get home."

"You know I'm gonna be concerned until I see that smile again."

"You saw it when I first got here."

"That wasn't your usual smile; that was a fake smile that put on to try to fool me."

"Guess I can't pull the wool over your eyes."

"That's right. You go ahead and get home so you can get some rest, you look pitiful baby."

Lauryn chuckles, "Alright, let me head up the road. It's good to see you doing this well James, you're almost back to your old self."

"Feels good too. Call me when you get home so that I know you made it safely."

"Yes sir."

Lauryn leaves the rehab center, gets in the vehicle and heads on home. She walks into her room, plops onto the bed, exhales deeply and finally gets under the covers. Just as she was about to close her eyes, she remembered that she had to call James.

"Just when you thought I was gonna forget about you," Lauryn said jokingly in that sleepy tone.

"I was getting worried. How you feelin' beautiful?"

"I thought I told you not worry about me. I'm fine; I told you I just need some rest."

"Well get your rest, I'm glad you made it home safely."

"Alright, have a good night."

"Night."

James was up for a little while recalling that event from junior year. What Lauryn didn't notice was that James had the look of exhaustion in his eyes, she didn't notice because she was exhausted herself, she didn't pay him too much mind this time. James was a little concerned about his chronic exhaustion, so he made a doctor's appointment. The next day, James himself wasn't feeling well, not that he was exhausted, not that Lauryn gave him anything because she was simply exhausted, but it was yet another episode like in the past.

Lauryn feels better after a good night's sleep and decides to go see James immediately after she got off work.

"You don't look so good James, you alright?"

"I feel like I did back in junior year."

"That's not good. How long has it been since you've felt this way?"

"I've been very tired lately; I hope I'm not catching anything."

"Well if it is something, hopefully it will pass quickly. You do look really sick; maybe you should go lie down and try getting some rest."

"You're right, I'm extremely exhausted, but I wanted to see you."

"You could've called me and told me you weren't feeling well and I would've went straight home, it's no big deal. But you need to go to bed, you look like you're about to fall out."

Lauryn looked with concern as she watched her old friend trudge his way to his room sluggishly. *I hope he's alright, if he feels any way like he looks, then I've got some praying to do.* James got back to his room and collapsed on his bed into a deep sleep and slept for several days uninterrupted. When Lauryn called to check on him, she always told the person who answered the phone not to wake him. She instructed the personnel, doctors, and his therapist not to make a big deal out of his long span of sleep. When he finally woke up, he was back on schedule, but he wasn't back to himself as of yet. He was missing his favorite girl, so he decided to give her a call.

"Hey beautiful."

"Heeeeeey, I didn't expect to hear from you until at least tomorrow. How you feelin'?"

"I've had better days, but I'm not complaining."

"I heard that."

"How are you?"

"I'm fine."

"You're still doing that, huh?"

"I can't help it, force of habit. But I really am doing alright, I promise. I caught up on my rest that night and was feeling better soon after."

"That's good."

"Yeah, but how are you feeling?"

"Not quite like myself, but I'm makin' it."

"Now that sounds like the James Willard that I know."

"I'm slowly getting back to James, I feel me coming back to myself."

"That's good."

"Next week is the week I can start going out…"

"Yes, and…?" Lauryn acted as if she didn't know what was coming next.

"I recall a certain someone making me a promise."

"That's right, I did and I will keep to my word. What day would you like to have lunch?"

"Whatever day I can fit into your schedule love."

"Hhhmmm, how about next Friday, we'll go to lunch."

"Sounds like a plan to me baby. I can't believe it, we're finally doing this thang."

Lauryn laughs and James has a certain twinkle in his eye as he hears his favorite girl do his favorite thing, laugh.

"I love to hear that laugh girl. I needed that."

"Something on your mind?"

"How could you tell over the phone?"

"I could tell in the tone of your voice."

James exhales deeply, "I'm just a little bothered about something…"

"What is it? You know you can tell me anything."

"I'm bothered at how sick I got…"

"I was rather concerned about you, this wasn't the first time it happened. Whether you know it or not, I've kept a closer eye on you think. I've noticed a pattern with you and your doctors and therapist have noticed as well. You've been really tired here lately and you've been moving slower."

"Girl, you still have your ways of stunning me."

"How so?"

"Your silent observations and how much you care."

"I'm always going to care."

"I'm glad to know that."

"You should've never forgotten it."

James sighs and there's a moment of silence. Lauryn takes that time to recollect on the comments that James's doctor has shared with her. She knows that there is a fundamental problem, but she can't quite place her finger on it, or maybe she doesn't want to. *I pray this is nothing too serious, he's doing so well and I don't know if he can bear any bad news right now.*

"I still don't understand it…but I want to thank you."

"For what?"

"For believing me after I've given you so many reasons not to, for sticking by me at every turn, for encouraging me, for being in my life as long as you have and staying in it, for helping me to help myself…for bringing me back to God."

"I'm not the one you should be thanking."

"Thank You God for ALL that You've done for me, second chance after second chance. When I know I don't deserve anything that You've done for me, You still came through at the perfect time and spared me from all destruction."

"Amen."

"But I am thankful for you though. You've brought so much light to many of my dark days."

"I could very well say the same thing."

"Oh, please."

"I'm serious, James."

"What exactly is it that I did for you? If I can recall correctly, you're the one who did for me the most, you were my rock, my shoulder to cry on, I talked your ears off, you prayed for me, you prayed over me, the list is endless what you've done for me, what have I done for you?"

"We've gone through this a million times James, it was your friendship. Your friendship pulled me out of a lot of dark days, your friendship helped me cope with being away from home because you brought home to me, and your friendship has stopped me from crying many tears."

"Ain't no way in the world I could've done all that. All I did was go to class with you, and we stayed up all night and talked, most of that was me talking about myself, we hung out from time to time…"

"Exactly."

"Wait what? I didn't do anything but show up."

"Exactly."

"I'm still confused."

"You gave me consistency, you came into my life and stuck around. Nobody who I called a friend stayed around unless they needed me for whatever reason."

"It's been my pleasure being in your life because it's been a blessing you being in mine."

"That's sweet."

"It's the truth."

"Well I don't want to keep you up, I'm glad you're at least feeling better. Get some rest."

"Thank you beautiful, I'm glad I called you."

"I'm glad you called me too. Good night."

"Good night, love."

Lauryn went to bed with a certain cheerful disposition that she even had a smile on her face when she went to sleep. James on the other hand, was still more worried than he seemed on the phone; his doctor's appointment was in the morning, so he decided to head to sleep.

James went to his doctor's appointment and finally got an explanation for everything that was happening. It was the worst news of his life. Not only did he find this out on the day of his therapy session, there was another significance to this dark day…it was the anniversary of the death of his mother. James needed something, anything to lift his spirits, luckily Lauryn promised to come visit him today. He dared not to share this news with her.

As Lauryn walked in, James couldn't help but to have a sad expression that he just couldn't hide this time.

"There's the most beautiful girl in the world. How are you?"

"Oh my goodness James, what's wrong?! You look like you're about to break down crying, is everything okay?"

Lauryn paused from all of her frantic questions as James hung his head low. *Oh no, I hope he didn't get too much bad news at the doctor's office today.* Lauryn positioned her head to James's, grabbed his hand with one hand and lifted his face with the other hand.

"What's wrong James?

James cries hysterically, and yet again Lauryn is left to do what she knows how to do best, she comforts him.

Chapter 3: A Sharp Left Turn

Oh my goodness, something is definitely wrong with James. I wonder what was told to him at his doctor's appointment. I could just go to the doctor and ask him, but I don't want to betray James by knowing, I'll let him tell me what's going on...whatever it is, I pray he gets through it all without going backward.

***

After James finally calms down, he looks at Lauryn with those blood-shot red eyes and saw her attentive look of concern and he breaks down again. Lauryn proceeds to comfort her old friend and awaits him to calm down once more. It got worse this time; James begins to hyperventilate and can't seem to catch his breath.

"Nurse! Doctor! Somebody! ANYBODY!"

At this point, James was unresponsive and Lauryn was in a frantic panic. *Lord, please help him breathe! He needs to calm down.*

Finally, an emergency response team arrives and gets James to a stable breathing pattern. Lauryn is present the whole time by his side to make sure that he'll be okay. *Thank God.* James is carried to the local hospital and kept for a couple of days for observation. Lauryn pays her old friend a visit while he's still admitted.

James peeps open his eyes.

"Well hello James Willard."

James fully opens his eyes in a sluggish manner and silently chuckles. "Lauryn Nevaeh Jones, you can surely make an entrance."

"How you doin'?"

James sighs "I'm alright."

"How you feelin'?"

"That's another story."

Lauryn looks at James intently as she did that day at the crack house.

"You look like something's on your mind, you alright?"

"There's always something on my mind girl, you know that."

"Yeah, I know, but it just seems like there's a specific something that's really getting to you. You know you can tell me anything. What's up?"

"I...I just..."

Lauryn looks at James and sees the trouble in his face, and it also seemed like he wasn't ready to tell her, or anyone for that matter. Lauryn grabs James's hand. "Shhhh...don't tell me if you don't want to, it's okay, tell me when you're ready, if you're ever ready."

"I just can't bring myself to do it right now."

"That's fine, just rest. I came here to see you and how you're doing; if you want me to leave so you can rest I will; it's not a problem."

James squeezes Lauryn's hand tightly. "Please, don't."

Lauryn saw the pain in his eyes and she agreed to stay as long as he wanted her to.

It's 2 a.m. and both Lauryn and James are still awake. "You need to get some rest, Law."

"I'm fine, I just want to be sure that you're alright."

James exhales. "You are truly something else. I don't deserve you in my life and here you are."

"I'll make you a deal: if you fall into a stable pattern of sleep, and I know you'll stay sleep, then I'll go home."

"Fine, but you need to rest Law. I know you have a lot on your plate with your job and the church. I feel really bad that you stayed here this long."

"Hey hey hey, don't worry about me and whatever's goin' on. You just worry about you and gettin' better."

"You still don't dwell on yourself I see."

"You got that right."

"But somebody has to be there for you darlin'."

"God got me."

"I heard that."

"So like I said, don't worry about me, you just worry about you getting better, getting out of this hospital, and getting out of rehab."

"I promise I don't deserve you in my life."

"If I weren't meant to have something to do with your life, I wouldn't be here."

James shakes his head as if he was in disbelief and he laughs.

"What's so funny Mr. Willard?"

"You are Ms. Jones."

"What about me is so hilarious?"

"Just you."

Lauryn gives James a side eye, "Alright then."

James sits back and reflects while Lauryn observes him.

"There you go again."

"What?"

"Your silent observations."

"I can't help it."

"What is it that you're observing when you're observing me?"

"Everything."

"Why?"

"Force of habit."

They both begin to laugh. In the midst of the laughter, the doctor comes in.

"I'll leave you two alone for a moment...Doctor." Lauryn gives the doctor a respectful head nod and leaves the room.

Once the doctor walks out the door, Lauryn walks back in and notices that James's mood has changed.

"What's wrong James?"

James shakes his head, looks away and starts fighting back tears. James got the confirmation of something he so prayed he wouldn't.
"Will you please just stay with me for as long as you can? I know you have to work, but please, as long as you can," James said shakily as he was crying.

"Of course I will. And I don't have to work tomorrow, tomorrow is Saturday. I'll be here with you as long as you need me."

"...thank you."

Lauryn knew that there was something terribly wrong, but she didn't want to force questions upon James, not right now.

Lauryn sat there gently stroking James's hand until he went to sleep about an hour later.

Lord Jesus, whatever is going on with James, let it be something that he can handle and get through without going backward. Heal him, Lord. Heal him…

Lauryn was up all night to be sure that James was sleep and stayed sleep; unfortunately, it was a rough night for James. He, the nurse, the doctor, and Lauryn were up through those wee hours of the morning and even into the afternoon until James got into a stable sleeping pattern.

It was about 9 p.m. Saturday evening, and James wakes up feeling just a little bit better.

"Don't tell me you've been awake all this time, Law."

"Don't worry 'bout all that, how you feelin'?"

"The absolute least amount better."

"Improvement is improvement. How are you though?"

James exhales, "Troubled."

"You mind sharing with the class what's on your mind?"

"I still can't."

"That's fine."

"But enough about me; how are you?"

"I'm sitting here looking at how pitiful you look, and you're asking me how I'm doing?"

"Yeah."

"I'm not the one in the hospital bed, sir."

James genuinely laughs for the first time since he's been in the hospital.

"There's a laugh."

Lauryn smiles and James has that twinkle in his eye that Lauryn sees for the first time.

"Girl, I just love it when you smile. You brighten up my day…you brighten up my life."

"A simple smile can't possibly do that James."

"You're right, but yours does."

Lauryn laughs heartily, "You think you *so* smooth."

"I try every now and then."

The doctor walks in once more with an austere visage and Lauryn leaves the room. James got some news that was worse than before, what he knew, became worse. Lauryn walks back into the room after the doctor walks out; James was expressionless. Lauryn walked up to James and hugged him.

"Whatever's going on, you know I'm here for you."

James remained silent and just hugged the tightest he's ever hugged anyone.

The next day, Lauryn had to preach so she left in the wee hours of the morning and had the nurse keep a constant eye on him and keep her up with his progress.

Lauryn's sermon was shorter than usual because she was beyond exhausted. Just as Lauryn got home, before she could even get comfortable, her phone rang unexpectedly. It was the hospital, James had been released.

Well, at least he'll be back at rehab where everybody can keep a close eye on him. Lord, please let him get through this, whatever the situation may be.

Lauryn was fast asleep after that phone call, and before she knew it, her alarm clock was going off for her to get up and get ready for work.

Lauryn went to work tired as ever, but that was nothing new, but there was something on her mind…James.

Lauryn decided to work through lunch and finally the day went by fast enough so that she could go home and rest. She walked her usual way like any other day, but there was something that threw off her rotation…

"Mm, mm, mm, why did God make you so fine! Girl, I know you not gone go past me without saying hi."

Lauryn stopped in utter shock, and she turned around…

"James?!"

Chapter 4: All Over Again

I can't believe this! I just knew he was going to stick with it this time. That news at the hospital must've been something serious for him to be back at his old place on that jagged rock in front of that old, raggedy crack house. Lord, please tell me you have a plan of action for him, he was doing so well, then this bad news. God, I know it was a test, but please give James the strength to endure it to the end.

***

"Oh sweetheart, you don't look too pleased to see me."

"You got that right."

"Why not?"

"James you know good and well why I'm not happy to see you here looking like this."

It was painfully evident by his appearance that James was high, and not coming down any time soon.

"I'm going to wait awhile for you to come back to yourself, then I'm coming back for you. And you better be here."

Lauryn had the most stern, disappointed, scolding look on her face when she was talking to James; in reality, she was heartbroken.

Time had passed to what Lauryn deemed was appropriate to go back and get James, and sure enough she was correct. She got out of her truck full of rage as she approached James.

Before she could say anything…

"I know."

"James, are you kidding me?! What's going on? You better start talking some sense into yourself."

"I know."

"James, I'm not going to argue with you, I won't even say another word to you, just get in the truck."

James followed suit and went back to the rehab facility and got himself back to his room. The news that James received at the hospital was major, his feeble heart and even weaker will couldn't take the severity of the news. Lauryn set up an appointment with James's therapist for James, and he went as instructed.
The therapy session was somewhat rejuvenating for James. Once Lauryn felt that James was back in the swing of things, she promised him a visit.

"I must be doin' something right."

"How you figure sir?"

"Cause you're here."

"Well, I figured I'd reward you for good behavior."

"Then I am doing something right."

"If that's how you want to put it, sure."

"I'll take it any way I can get it. I'm glad to see you."

"I'll see if I feel the same way later on."

"No slack huh?"

"Never."

"Okay, I deserve that. Can you at least tell me how you're doing?"

"I'm fine."

"Are you sure? You look beyond exhausted."

"I'm fine."

"Reverend Lauryn Nevaeh Jones, J. D., why can't you seem to ever tell me what's really going on?"

"You had to add my titles like that?"

"As a matter of fact, yes I did."

"What was your purpose?"

"Because I wanted you to take heart into everything that you are. I'm sure you've got to be one of the youngest, if not, the youngest partner at that firm and with a J. D. You have a beautiful church that you're the head of and your congregation loves you. Give, that's all you do, give give give. For as long as I can remember, that's what you've always done. But who gives to you Law?"

"There was this one guy, I knew him in high school and in college…then we lost touch for ten years."

"I wonder what happened to that charismatic guy with a plan of a future."

"You tell me."

James exhaled and changed the subject, "We never went out on our date."

"If I recall correctly, that entire weekend was spent at the hospital."

"That's right, so do I get a do over?"

"You've backslid, you now you have to work your way back to that point. When you make it there again…we'll cross that bridge when we get to it."

"I'm just completely amazed."

"At what?"

"You…and God."

"Elaborate."

"I've let you down, and you're still here for me. I was in the worst mental state that weekend, and that's what made me back slide. But here you are, you came and got me out of my moment of weakness, and built me back up. I know I hurt you in the process, and I deeply apologize for it all, but I'm so thankful that you still believe in me enough to force me back here when I was at my weakest. Anybody else would've given up on me."

"How many times do I have to tell you, I'm not your average woman? I've been telling you this for over fifteen years."

"It finally awakened in my mind though, I really believe you. You are truly one of a kind, you're caring, intelligent, beautiful, wise, you have this love for God that amazes me to a point where I want to get to know God more. I'm just sorry that no man has come to realize how amazing you are."

"I'm not concerned about the thoughts of man, just the thoughts of my God."

"See, just like that. God carries such a pertinent part of your heart that any man who isn't deserving of you, God will shun him away from you to protect you."

"God got me like that."

"I realize that full well now."

"Why'd it take you so long?"

"I don't know."

James was left to ponder that thought, he had known Lauryn for almost twenty years, including the time of each other's absence.

"Well James, I'm glad to see you back on track. You have a good evening."

"Bye beautiful."

Another week has passed, and once again, James gets some more bad news. What he thought was bad before, was not close to the news that he received. This bad news sent him spiraling into another depression similar to the previous episode, but it was worse this time. What Lauryn didn't know about that day at the crack house is, James told the dealer to hold that huge fix for as long as he possibly could and that he would be paying on it his usual way. James made an unmonitored call to his dealer, and told him to get his special fix ready.

The next day after that unmonitored phone call, James was nowhere to be found.

Lauryn went to work as she usually did. Today went by exceptionally slow and she was swamped with work. She was so swamped that she worked six hours over time. She was so far beyond exhausted, she couldn't see straight. She went past that old, raggedy crack house as usual, but once again, something wasn't so usual about that day...

"HEY BABY!!!"

Lauryn stopped in her tracks, turned around, wiped her eyes and did a double take. *Lord, this better be a hallucination or I'm gonna kill this man...*

"C'mon baby, you not gone speak?!"

James was extra loud and extra obnoxious. It was painfully evident that James was high as ever.

"James, please tell me that I'm just seeing things 'cause I'm tired."

"Naw baby, this is the real deal right here!"

Lauryn decided she wasn't going to wait for him to sober up this time. "James, get in the truck...NOW."

James began to laugh, "We finally goin' on that date baby?"

James was unstable as he was standing, he was wobbling all over the place, it was almost as if he couldn't even see straight...which he probably couldn't.

"James, if you don't get in this SUV, I promise you that you will regret every move you make afterward."

"I thought preachers weren't supposed to be violent," James said with slurred language and he began to lean closer to Lauryn.

Lauryn pulled James as hard as she could, she then realized that she didn't need all of her strength to drag him; come to find out, James was light as a feather when he was high.

Lauryn pushed him into her vehicle and got in herself.

"James, I don't understand it, you know you can talk to me about any and everything but instead you decide to backslide AGAIN. I thought you were forreal this time, but I clearly see I was wrong about that. Nope, not this time…you're not getting away again. No more phone calls, PERIOD. No visitation, none of that. You will only see the light of day to exercise, and I might restrict you to the gym. You sir, are officially on lockdown."

James laughs hysterically and continues to look out the window.

They arrive at the rehab facility where there is security, the doctor with a sedative, and three nurses waiting. As if on cue, before the needle even touched his skin, James falls flat on the concrete. The overdose was officially starting to take hold of James's system.

Lord, what now?

An emergency response team was on the scene fortunately, and James was immediately taken care of. He was rushed to the hospital.

Some time had passed before Lauryn could get an answer on James's condition. The doctor confirmed that he had overdosed to a point of mortality.

This can't be! Lord, please help him back to his earth…I know he's not done serving on this earth.

James was in critical condition for about a month, and was finally induced into a coma. In the induced coma, he was finally in stable condition; unfortunately, the coma lasted far longer than anticipated...James was in a coma for three months practically brain dead. James had become a vegetable with little to no hope of coming out of the coma.

Lord, I just need you to pull him through this. I know it's been a long time coming, but it's time for him to live again.

One miraculous day, James's heart rate began to increase into a normal heart rate. Soon after, James opened his eyes.

Oh my goodness! God, You did it again! Thank You, Lord! To God be all the glory!

Lauryn alerted the nurse and the doctor that he had awakened.

James turned his head and Lauryn told him not to move too much. Just as James tries to speak... "Shh, don't try to speak right now."

James smiled as Lauryn sat there comforting him, he couldn't believe she had stuck by him through all of this.

The doctor and the nurse came to tend to him and had reported that he was recovering in a miraculously swift manner.

Thank You, Lord. You've done it again.

Lauryn went to the hospital to visit her old friend; James was sitting up and looked lively.

Chapter 5: For Real THIS Time

"Such a beautiful sight for such sore eyes."

"Hello, Mr. Willard."

"How are you beautiful?"

"You beat me to the punch; I was getting ready to ask you the same question."

"If I answer you honestly, will you answer me honestly?"

"We'll see."

James knew full well that he couldn't get through to Lauryn. "I'm starting to feel better, and I'm so glad that you're here."

"I'm fine."

"I knew that was coming."

"Which makes me wonder why you continue to ask."

"Because it's the gentlemanly thing to do."

"Oh yeah, you're feeling better."

James chuckled, "Hey, at least I tried."

"How are you James?"

"I'm great now that I know you're here."

"I've been here."

"Really?" Once again, James was simply amazed.

"Don't seem so shocked, sir."

"But I am."

"Why?"

"Because I've done nothing to deserve your friendship. You've been my backbone through all of this. I've done nothing but disappoint you and you're still standing strong by my side."

"Well you should've known that you couldn't get rid of me James."

James sat back and reflected. His thoughts took him back to after undergrad when they split up, and realized that she was his guardian angel.

"What are you thinking about over there?"

"You."

"Come again?"

"You heard me, I'm thinking about you."

"But I'm sitting right here," Lauryn said in a joking manner, but there was some seriousness to the situation.

"I was thinking about you in the past."

"How far back we talkin'?"

"Ten years ago..."

There was a moment of grave silence; suddenly the air seemed to shift with the vibe of the conversation. Lauryn knew that James couldn't bear but to be in a specific state emotionally but so long, so she decided to change the subject.

"So I hear you're coming out of here soon."

"Law?"

"Yes?" Lauryn immediately had a look of concern on her face; she turned herself to face him completely and was ready to listen intently.

James shook his head, "I just don't get it."

"What do you mean?"

"Why am I still alive? What's my purpose now? I-I've messed up so...many...times, I just..."

"Before you continue, let me tell you something – look at me..."

James uncovered his face to reveal his bloodshot eyes to look at Lauryn.

"Your purpose is not yet fulfilled on this earth. God has set forth for you to do some good, this is your chance. Obviously, God believes in your vision so much that He let you live through this. I wasn't going to tell you this, but the day that you woke up was the day that they were gonna pull the plug. You have no next of kin, so they were gonna do it at will with no consent of anyone; God woke you up in the nick of time. God ain't through with you yet James."

James could do nothing but cry.

Lauryn was there by his side through all the tears that day, and decided to stay with him all day.

"Ya know I put you on lockdown right?"

"Huh?"

"When I went to get you that day, I put you on lockdown: no phone calls, visits, none of that."

"But you're here."

"I had to give you some incentive for your progress."

"Well I appreciate it."

"You're welcome."

James looks at Lauryn and shakes his head.

"Why are you shaking your head at me sir?"

"Because."

"Because...?"

"Just because."

"Alright then."

There was a moment of silence, but the mood was very light.

"Shouldn't you be at work Law?"

"I decided to stay with you for the remainder of the day."

"You're skipping work for me?"

"If that's how you want to put it, sure."

"You make me feel so special."

"Oh stop, it's not that deep."

"But it is though."

"How you figure?"

Lauryn already knew the answer to that question; she just wanted to know if James was going to repeat himself.

"Every. Single. Time...every single time I mess up, I just lose it and I want to give up. Then God tells me that I can't, and you tell me that I can't. But I can't believe after all of this, you're still here for me, and God still finds that there is some good in this old, battered heart of mine."

"Trouble don't last always, James. You have to remember that. God has been ordering your steps all along, even at every detour, He planned your escape. You gotta know that you're on this earth to do some good James. If God didn't see you fit to serve Him, you would've left this earth a long time ago."

"I guess I just can't seem to grasp that concept."

"God loves us all James, and if He didn't feel your sincerity, you wouldn't have been given second, third, fourth, and so on chances."

"God, I'm so blessed. Thank You, Lord for bringing through the storms."

It was at that moment that James decided nothing was going to stop him THIS time, he was going to finish rehab and make something of himself. More than that, he was going to become the man that God made him to be.

About a week later, James awoke from what was the most rejuvenating sleep of his life, and it was time for him to go back to the rehab center. When he got there, he had an unexpected visitor.

"Well well well, and what do I owe for this sight of beauty?"

"Let's just say I'm glad to see you've returned to this specific place."

"I told you Law, THIS time will be different."

Lauryn just looked at James.

"You don't believe me."

"It's not that I don't believe you James, we just gotta take this thing one day at a time."

"I'm okay with that."

"There's something different about you James, I don't know what it is, but I'm lovin' it."

"When I was in that coma and when I was sleep all last week, I did a lot of thinking and talking to God."

Lauryn looked at James very nonchalantly. "Really now."

"You don't believe me."

"It's not that I don't believe you James, it's just that we need to take this one day at a time."

"That's very fair. I can deal with that."

"I believe IN you, James. I just don't know to what extent I can trust you."

"That's also fair."

"One day at a time, James."

James exhales deeply, "One day at a time…"

Chapter 6: Divine Epiphany

It's been about two weeks since James and I had that talk. I hope he wasn't too discouraged with what I said to him, but Lord, what else could I say but the truth? I haven't talked to him since that day; I wonder how he's doing. I think I'll pay him an impromptu visit.

***

"And what do I owe for this visage of beauty? You are lookin' mighty fine today Ms. Jones."

"Well you don't look too shabby yourself Mr. Willard. How are you?"

"Fantastic."

"Really now."

"That's right."

"Well good, I'm glad."

"I'm so happy to see you. I've truly missed you."

"Is that so?"

"Yes ma'am."

"Well, you sound better, you look A LOT better. Maybe I need to separate from you more often."

"Please don't."

Lauryn laughed and even decided to give James a hug.

"A hug too? HALLELUJAH!"

Lauryn laughed even harder this time. "Yeah, a hug too."

"What did I do to deserve that?"

"I'm just proud of you, that's all."

"Girl, don't start with all that, you gone have me cryin' up in here."

"I'm serious though James, you're doing really well."

"I'm tryin' to get to that stage again so we can go on that date we never went on."

"I knew you had a motive."

"Well, you're the one that keeps me goin'. Thinking about that date, just fills me with joy and makes me want to work harder so I can get to that place."

"As long as there is something positive that keeps you going, and not something negative. I'm really proud of you, James."

"Thank you, Law."

"You're welcome."

After a few more moments, they said a few more words and parted ways. James was the happiest he had been in a very, very long time. He felt as though they were back in college again, everything was everything.

Lauryn went home thinking that she was getting her old best friend back. She couldn't believe that James was moving the way he was. What was so significant about a platonic outing? After that question popped into her head, Lauryn began to wonder. Was there more to the jokes? Was he really joking? Does he feel more than he says?

The following Saturday, Lauryn decided to stay in, clean up, and relax. She hadn't had a day off in a little while so she wanted to take full advantage of it. While she was resting, she called a few of her church members to check on them and see how they were feeling. As soon as Lauryn finds out that something's wrong with one of her members, she's quick to find out what's going on. Lauryn's members lover her, not only as a pastor, but as a person. She's come into acquaintance with many of her members and has formed strong bonds.

As if on cue, as soon as Lauryn was finished with her last phone call, she received a phone call herself from her good friend, James.

"Hello?"

"Hey beautiful."

"You always say that."

"Because I like for you to know what you are, you are beautiful. The most beautiful girl in the world."

"I see somebody's having a good day. What's up?"

"Nothing, just wanted to hear your voice, it's been a little while."

"What's really going on, sir?"

"You saw through me once again, that's why you're so good at what you do. What would that firm do without you there?"

"They're gonna find out in a few years when I establish my firm. But I love my job though."

"That's good."

"Alright James, come on now, what's really going on?"

"Okay, okay. I've excelled with the program, and I'm coming to a point where I can start coming to church again."

"That's great; some of my members have been asking where you've disappeared off to."

"I was wondering if you took sermonic requests?"

"That depends…"

"On what?"

"On if it has to do with the sermon that I've already prepared and if I can tie the two together. I have a strong feeling though, that you want me to speak on healing, and that's already my sermon for tomorrow."

"How did you know that I was gonna ask you to speak on healing?"

"I speak on what the spirit leads me to speak on, James. Plus, there's a lot going on with some of my members and I think they need to hear a good word on healing."

"Wow."

"What is wow sir?"

"I'm just amazed at how God works."

"God does work in amazing ways."

"Law?"

"Yes sir."

"Thank you."

"What are you thanking me for?"

"Thank you for being here for me, thank you for being kind even when I've hurt you. Thank you for sticking with me all these years. Thank you caring about me, thank you for letting me know the truth all the time. Thank you for the tough love and pushing me forward. Thank you for loving me, thank you for praying for me…thank you for even leaving a piece of your heart for me. You have no idea what kind of strength you have given me over time, you're the reason why I keep going, you're the reason why I have a hope for tomorrow, you're the reason why I believe in God, you're the reason why I constantly pray. It's because of you and God that I'm trying to become a better me."

"God is directing you James; I have nothing to do with that."

"But you're the person who's been giving me the moral support."

"I do what the spirit leads me to do, James. Plus, we've known eachother for eighteen years; that accounts for something. Yes James, I care for you. In the past, you were my backbone, you kept me going, I'm returning the favor."

James was facially expressionless and was at a loss for words.

"Law?"

"Yes?"

"Can I ask you a question?"

"Anything."

"Will you ever give up on me?"

"No, I won't. But I have a question for you James."

"What's that?"

"Will you stop giving up on yourself?"

James sat there stunned at Lauryn's question; everything was quiet for about a minute. Lauryn had to be sure that James had not hung up the phone.

"James?"

"I'm still here."

"You alright?"

"I'm fantastic now. You just helped me to solve my life's issue. Ever since graduation and everything happened, I've been the one constantly telling myself that I wasn't good enough. I wasn't good enough to move on in life, I wasn't good enough to even try, and I wasn't good enough for life itself. These past ten years have been so dark, and I've been the one bringing my own self down."

This was the grandest epiphany that James has ever had. James went on to thank Lauryn and God for what became the fire in him to move completely on with the program. Before they hung up, Lauryn offered to pray over James and of course James agreed. The two shared a very emotional prayer and hung up.

The following Sunday, Lauryn was on fire and she set the entire church ablaze preaching on healing. It seemed almost as if healing was the magic word that day; all she had to do was say the word one time and the spirit just moved within the entire congregation, even the musicians and those who were listening to the sermon elsewhere in the building.

After service, just like in the past, each and every single person in the congregation hugged Lauryn saying things like "Good job, Reverend" and "That was so on time for me, thank you so much" and "God bless you Reverend, what a powerful word." James was the very last person to approach Lauryn at the end of the service, she was very happy to see him.

"That sermon was the truth, Law."

"God is the truth, so I can't do nothing but tell the truth."

"God is so good."

"Yes, He is. How you doin' James?"

"I feel completely rejuvenated."

"To God be the glory, that's great James."

"Yes ma'am."

"You want a ride back to the rehab center?"

"That would be great."

"Alright, follow me to my office so I can gather my things and we can get out of here."

"Don't you have to wait around for a while?"

"That's the perk of being the boss James; you can leave when you feel like it. I trust my various ministry staff to do what they need to do, the quicker they work, the quicker they leave as well."

"Mm mm mm, a true leader."

"I try to lead, but sometimes it all doesn't work out the way that it should. But most of the time, things run smoothly."

By the time Lauryn finished her statement, they were in her office and she was gathering her things getting ready to leave.

"Beautiful office you have here. The mahogany finish is a nice touch."

"Thank you."

"Your favorite color is still black I see."

"That is correct."

"You see, I still remember some of your favorite things."

"I would hope you do."

James chuckled, "well, as fried as my brain has been in the past you know ten years, I'm surprised I remember my own name."

"There's some truth to that. But you're really blessed, James."

"I sure am."

"A lot of people in your predicament wouldn't even be alive right now."

"I'm beyond blessed."

"I'm glad to know that you acknowledge God the way you do."

"Of course. If I didn't, I would be like the others…dead. I thank God for it all. I thank God for you."

Lauryn took a long, hard look into James's face. "James, you're gonna make it through this."

James hung his head. "I'm trying to get to a place where I can find confidence in myself."

"You'll get there, until then; you know you can count on me to give you encouragement. And not even just me, you know you got the staff at the center and the church."

"It really gives me comfort and great joy to know that I actually have some stable support."

"There's always gonna be some form of stable support James. You just have to seek it."

"Thank you."

After that, they left church and headed to the rehab facility. James got out of the vehicle, but before he shut the door once more, he said, "Thank you."

"I'm here."

James smiled and went inside of the center.

Lauryn smiled as she watched James go inside of the center. *Thank You, Lord.* As soon as she's about to pull off, she gets a phone call. The phone call is from the hospital, one of her members has been in an awful car accident. She rushed to the hospital right away to check on the member. Lauryn's church member was in such bad shape, Lauryn stayed at the hospital for days praying over her member and finally her member came through and Lauryn went home. Lauryn was so tied up with her church member, she almost forgot about James. As soon as Lauryn gets a moment's breath from working and being with her church member, she called James and checked on him.

"Well, well, well, didn't think I'd ever hear from you again."

"I know, I've been super busy. I'm sorry I haven't called sooner. How are you, James?"

"I'm doing great, I can now have phone calls unmonitored."

"That's wonderful James."

"You alright beautiful? You sound so exhausted."

"I'm always exhausted, you know that."

"Well you sound extra exhausted."

"Kinda."

"What's going on?"

"I'm not about to bombard your ears."

"I insist you tell me."

"Fine. One of my members got into a fatal car accident and I've been going over to the hospital every day after work. Along with all of that, I'm handling her case and it just so happened that right before I called you, I just got off the phone with her doctor and she's sick. So I'll be over there in a few to pray over her some more; she really needs any prayer she can get. If you could pray for her please, that would make a world of a difference."

"Of course I'll pray for her, but I'll also be praying for you darlin', you got a lot going on."

"I didn't mean to talk your ear off."

"No trouble, love."

"Thank you for praying for her. She's been through some things."

"I'm actually able to go for very short outings, would you mind I come with you one day to pray for her?"

"Of course I don't mind, both of us would love that. Thank you so much, James. I really appreciate that."

"Of course."

"I called to check on you and you haven't talked about you yet."

"I have to be sure that my girl is okay first."

"I'm fine, James."

"Promise me that you won't run yourself down."

"I'll try not to. Now back to you…you're able to go out besides church now?"

"Not for long, ten to thirty minutes."

"Improvement is improvement. How you been feeling lately?"

"Great."

"That's good. You sound really strong, James. I'm proud of you."

"That really means a lot coming from you."

"Why?"

"I very much so value your opinions, compliments, and wisdom…I always have."

"It's nice to know that somebody values me."

"And I always will."

Lauryn smiled. "It's getting late, James. You go ahead and get some rest. I'm so overjoyed that you're doing alright and I'm so proud of you."

"Thank you so much. You're making me feel like I'm doing something right."

"You are, you're getting your life back."

"And it feels so good."

"Good night, James."

"Sweet dreams, beautiful."

After they hung up, James went to bed as Lauryn suggested and Lauryn went up to the hospital. By the time Lauryn got to the hospital, it was after midnight. Her church member finally opened her eyes for the first time and Lauryn was right there when she opened her eyes holding her hand. *Thank You God, for once again blessing her with life.* Not too much longer after she opens her eyes, she has a coughing attack. The nurse and doctor run in to the rescue and Lauryn was to the side praying the whole time. Once she was stabilized, Lauryn went back over to her church member, held her hand, and prayed.

The next morning came, and Lauryn snuck away to work. Her church member was stable thankfully and was ready for surgeries. While Lauryn was at work, she got about three new cases while working on the two she already had. It was going to be a long day for Lauryn, she knew she was going to pull some massive overtime today.

Thankfully, about midday, she cracked her three new cases, turned them in to her boss, and went back to the case she was working on. A couple hours later, her office phone was ringing, it was the rehab facility. Lauryn was so hoping that nothing was wrong with James. She answered the phone very tentatively preparing for the worst, but praying for the best.

"Hello?"

"Hey beautiful."

Lauryn let out a deep sigh of relief, *Thank God.* "Hey James, you have no idea how much terror I was just filled with, I thought something was wrong. How are you?"

"I'm good. I called to check on you, I figured you'd still be at work this time of day."

"Yeah, I am. I'm fine, just getting a case together. What's up?"

"Nothing, I was just thinking about you."

"That's sweet, and it was really sweet of you to call me."

"I'm always thinking about you. How's your church member doing?"

"She's finally stable enough to go into surgery."

"Prayer works."

"By the grace of God, it sure does. And thank you again for praying for her, she needs all the prayer she can get. She lives by herself, no family, the church is pretty much all she has."

"I'll be sure to pray for her comfort."

"Thank you."

"No problem beautiful."

"You know, you've really been in your right mind here lately. Whatever you're doing, keep doing it."

"I told you, once you and I had that talk in your office at church, it was a divine epiphany that hit me and has kept me going all this time. And you've kept me going, of course."

"Haha, I'm flattered."

"But I've been telling you that for years."

"Yeah, you have. I can't deny that. I'm glad you're getting back to yourself, James. I've missed you."

"I've missed you too. I'm so glad to be getting back to myself."

There was a moment of silence.

"Well beautiful, I'll let you get back to working hard. I just wanted to check on you."

"Would you like to come pray this evening? She's having her first surgery tonight, and I think she would like the extra prayer and support."

"Sure."

"Great."

"You're making me feel all important and special. Because of God, you, and this rehab, I get to pray over something of importance."

"You pray over something of importance every day, James. Whenever you pray for yourself, you are praying over something of importance. You are important to God, and I know He's important to you."

"Wow, you're right. I've never really seen myself of somebody of importance though."

"Of course you're important, James."

"Thank you."

"For what?"

"For giving me my self-worth and giving me significance."

"You've always had significance, James, you've just never realized it."

"You're right."

James pondered over that as Lauryn ended the conversation so that she could get back to work. Before she hung up, she let James know what time to be ready. James recognized that the time that Lauryn gave her was a time later than the time she usually gets off work, and Lauryn was stunned at how James has paid attention over time.

The time came for Lauryn to go get James, and as suggested, James was ready and waiting.

"Look at you, on time and what not."

"I couldn't keep y'all waiting."

"Good. Ready?"

"Ready when you are."

"Alright, let's hit it."

The short ride to the hospital was silent as Lauryn was concentrating and preparing her heart and mind, and James was preparing as well.

"James, are you ready for this?"

With confidence, he said, "You bet."

They went inside, to the woman's room and all linked hands. Lauryn insisted that James start the prayer off and without hesitation he had a very strong start and Lauryn went on for a strong, emotional finish. Right after the prayer had concluded, it was time for the woman to go into surgery. Lauryn took James back to the rehab center and promised to keep him updated.

Once Lauryn got back to the hospital she waited for the surgery to end; luckily, she brought her work along with her and she was working on the case for the entirety of the surgery. Just as Lauryn was about to nod off into sleep, the doctor tapped Lauryn on the shoulder and said that the surgery was a success. Lauryn went in to see her; as Lauryn was walking in, her church member was slowly opening up her eyes and so delighted to see Lauryn that she shed a tear. Lauryn wiped away the tear, smiled, held her hand and prayed. After the prayer, Lauryn sat there as her church member drifted off into a blissful sleep. Lauryn knew her church member was excited to see Lauryn; what's so special about this church member is, she doesn't have any family, they're all deceased or very, very distant. Once Lauryn met her acquaintance, she was sure to reassure her member that she would always be there for her and would gladly call her family.

After a very brief conversation with her church member, Lauryn called James to update him as she promised.

"Hey there beautiful."

"Hello Mr. Willard, how are you?"

"I'm doin' just fine."

"That's good."

"How are you my lovely blossom?"

"You already know the answer to that question."

"Still thought I'd ask."

"That's sweet, but I didn't call you just to check on you. I also called to update you on my church member."

"Oh yeah, how's she doin'?"

"She's in alright shape, she came through the surgery and it was successful. She's resting now."

"That's good."

"Yeah. So, have you been resting enough James? You sound a little tired."

"Yes ma'am. I was actually getting ready to ask you the same question. You sound exhausted."

"You know sleep hasn't been in my vocabulary since college."

"That's because you've spent so much time taking care of everybody else except yourself. When are you gonna make time for you Law?"

"I have my me time."

"I don't believe you."

"But I do. Whenever I pray, that's me time."

"Aren't you praying for other people when you're praying?"

"Yes, I am. That doesn't matter though, it's still time to myself, just me and God."

"Can't argue with you there."

There is a pause as Lauryn gets called to the room by the nurse.

"Hey James, I hate to end the conversation right now, but I'm needed. I'll talk to you soon."

"I completely understand. I'm looking forward to your call."

"Alright, bye-bye."

"Bye."

Lauryn was called into the room because her church member woke up unexpectedly and saw that Lauryn wasn't there. Lauryn immediately reassured her church member that she had not gone anywhere and won't go anywhere as long as she needs her there. After Lauryn's church member finally calmed down, she fell asleep and Lauryn sat there and prayed.

Lauryn's church member stayed sleep for the remainder of the night and most of the following day. In the duration of the time that her church member was sleep, Lauryn was busy working on caseloads. From the time Lauryn left work, to about six hours later, Lauryn received three more cases. Fortunately for Lauryn, these were easy open and shut cases, so she solved them with some rather swiftness.

Once Lauryn's church member was comfortable enough, Lauryn left for work.

It was a fairly easy day for Lauryn, she spent most of the time working on the case of her church member and she even got off of work on time. As soon as she got in her vehicle, Lauryn received a phone call, it was her church member. The phone conversation was very brief but Lauryn was shocked as to how well her church member was doing. After she hung up with her church member, Lauryn decided to give James a call.

"Well hello, Reverend."

"How's it going James?"

"Better now I'm hearing the sound of your voice."

"Oh, and what was wrong before?"

"I've just been a little tired and sluggish."

"Yeah, I can tell. You feelin' alright?"

"I'm fine beautiful."

"If you say so, sir."

"So what's up, how are you?"

"I'm fine. I called to check on you and update you about my church member."

"How's she doing?"

"She's much stronger. Sitting up, breathing on her own, feeling better, she's really doing well."

"That's great."

"She asked about you."

"Me?"

"Yes, you."

"What did she have to say about lil ole me?"

"She wanted me to extend her most gracious thanks to you for that wonderful prayer."

"Aw shucks, it wasn't all that."

"You really did a good job James, I'm proud of you and I definitely know God is too."

"Thank you."

"You're welcome."

"Guess what!"

"What?"

"I've come to a point now where I can go out and come back as I please as long as I'm back by my curfew and I still make all of my appointments."

"That's great, James! I'm so proud of you. This is perfect actually, my church member wants to see you again; she wants to thank you in person."

"She wants to see me?"
"She sure does. I think she might have a thing for you."

"Why me? I have teeth missing and my brain is halfway fried…"

"Stop right there James. She sees your personality, she sees your heart. I'm tellin' you, I think she has a thing for you."

"She can't possibly be feeling anything for me. I think you're off this time, Law."

"Really now. Why don't we go find out?"

"What are you saying?"

"She wants to see you, remember?"

"But that was a one-time thing."

"Well, she requested to see you today. Do you wanna let her down?"

"I suppose not."

"Alright, well I'm getting off late again tonight, so…whatever the time I told you to be ready the last time, be ready at that time."

"Okay."

Both Lauryn and James happened to remember what time to be ready, so Lauryn wrapped up her work and went on to pick up James.

After Lauryn picked James up, they went to the hospital. As soon as they got to her room, Lauryn's church member perked right up and spoke before Lauryn or James had a chance to. Lauryn spoke briefly to her church member before her church member became completely engrossed in conversation with James. The conversation got so good, that James was so bold as to ask Lauryn's church member if she would like his company for the remainder of the time that she was in the hospital and she gratefully agreed.

Once Lauryn's church member got out of the hospital, she offered to take James out for a meal of appreciation for being there for her. After their outing, James and Lauryn's church member began to see each other regularly; she would either come see him at the rehab facility, he would make a voyage to see her, or they would see each other at church.

In the time of this little courtship, James would rarely call Lauryn and Lauryn didn't visit the rehab facility because she was afraid of interrupting their time together. Little did Lauryn know, that little attraction they had for each other was starting to fade away. One day, James noticed that he hadn't talked to Lauryn in quite some time, and he decided to call her, to talk to her and do a little venting.

"Well, well, well, I just knew you forgot about a sistah. How you doin', James?"

"I'm alright."

"Just alright? Every time I try to catch you at church, you're all hugged up with your boo or y'all are talking; I would think you'd be doing wonderfully."

"We've been having some problems here lately."

"Really? What's going on?"

"I mean, we still have a wonderful time together, but that certain something just isn't there like it was at the very beginning. She doesn't see me the way that she used to."

"Ah, I think I know what's going on here."

"Could you please enlighten a brotha?"

"Don't get me wrong James, you are a wonderful guy, but what I think happened was that she saw you as her superhero which made her cling to you so closely. Remember when I told you she had nobody? You became her somebody and she fell for you that way; now that you're not needed, for lack of better phrase, she doesn't see you the same way anymore."

"I see."

"Don't be so down on yourself James, you are a wonderful guy, and I'm sure you enjoyed having other company other than me around for a little while. And I know it felt great to date, and she didn't even judge you."

"You're right about some things Law, I did enjoy the dating and she didn't judge me, but you'll always be my favorite company and I'll never get tired of you."

"Oh stop. But do you see what's happening here?"

"Yeah I do. She told me she was coming by later to talk to me, I think we're breaking up."

"Aaww, I'm sorry to hear that James. You gonna be alright?"

"Yeah, I will be. But I'll call you after she leaves. I just wanted to call you since I haven't talked to you in so long. I miss you."

"I miss you, too."

"Talk to you later."

"Alright."

What James predicted was absolutely correct, Lauryn's church member came to break up with James. That conversation was full of compassion, she kept apologizing and telling James how appreciative of him she was. When she was getting ready to leave, she started to tear up, but James reassured her that no feelings were hurt and no harm was done. They hugged, and she left. After she left, James went to his room and called Lauryn back as he promised he would.

"Hey there."

"I called it."

"She broke up with you?"

"Yeah."

"You okay?"

"Yeah, I'm fine. No harm, no foul."

"I'm glad you're taking this as well as you are. I'm proud of you."

"Thank you. When I called you earlier, I never asked you how you're doing. How are you? How you been?"

"I'm fine, been tired lately as usual. Speaking of her, her court date is coming up. I finally got her case finished, it's solid. She'll be well compensated."

"That's great, I know she'll like that, and she rightfully deserves it."

"You sure you're alright James?"

"I'm a little sad, but I'll be fine."

"You know I'm here for you. You wanna talk about it?"

"Sure. I just, I thought this was actually gonna be something, ya know? I mean, I feel great to have been her superhero, but I just wish those subconscious feelings were real. She's so great, but I know she'll find someone better deserving of her."

"Don't put yourself down like that, James. You are truly a great guy. God is just preparing you for your wife, she's coming, and she'll be deserving of you and you of her."

"I don't deserve a good woman as broke down as I am."

"Don't say that James. Look at how far you've come. I'm so proud of you, I just smile every time I get a progress report from the facility or you call me and you sound better and better, stronger and stronger. And don't get me started on your faith, I can tell that your faith has grown so much, what woman wouldn't be proud of that?"

"I guess, but what about my past? I've done so much wrong..."

"Stop right there. The past is the past James, I'm sure whoever God has ordained as your wife will lovingly accept your past and see the present person that it made you to be."

"Thank you."

"You're welcome. Hey guess what?"

"What?"

"I have a couple surprises for you."

"Oh Lord."

"Haha, don't be afraid James. Surprise number one is, I pulled some strings with the advancement center, and you're gonna start taking some classes to refresh your memory of that degree which is still in-tact."

"Law, you are too much."

"But wait, that's not all. Surprise number two is…drum roll please…I called in a favor to a dentist friend of mine, you're gonna get a new set of choppers placed where the old ones used to be."

"Law, quit playin' with me girl."

"I'm serious, James. All of this is happening."

"I'm speechless, Law. I don't know how I can ever thank you girl?"

"You don't ever have to thank me for any of this James. You deserve all of this. Consider these things gifts from me and the rehab facility to you."

"I'm still speechless."

"I'll let you soak it in. But before I say good night, one more thing. We never went on our date sir. How about this, I'll come pick you up during my lunch hour and we'll have lunch. Sound like a plan?"

"You're tryin' to give me a heart attack aren't you? A date with you Law?"

"Haha, I figured you might like that, and maybe our lunch date tomorrow will help you take your mind off things."

"Most definitely. Thank you so much Law."

"What I just tell you about that thank you stuff?"

"I'm going to thank you anyway Law, this is so huge to me."

"Well you try to catch your breath and get some rest, I'll see you tomorrow."

"Yes ma'am! See you tomorrow. Sweet dreams beautiful."

"Good night Mr. Willard."

Lauryn felt so full to be a blessing to James and help to give him a second chance at life.

Lord, You did it again. Thank You God for letting James not only wage war but weather every storm thus far and lead him toward the victory. Lord, You are SO awesome.

James went to bed reassured that somebody on this earth wanted to see him do good, better in fact. He was also reassured that there is a God that's looking after him. James spent his entire prayer that night thanking God for Lauryn.

The next day, it came time for Lauryn's lunch hour and James was patiently awaiting Lauryn's arrival.

"Hey stranger, you ready to get some lunch?"

"Hey beautiful, yes I am. I saved my appetite just for this occasion."

"You look great James."

"I feel great."

"Wonderful."

"So where are we going for lunch?"

"To the old favorite spot."

"Perfect."

"You look a lil tired James, you alright?"

"Yeah, I was so excited by the news you gave me last night, and the thought I would get to see you today and we're finally going on this date, I just couldn't sleep."

"Sure, sure."

"I'm serious Law."

"If you say so."

"I've really been missing you."

"I've missed you too. I've been missing our conversations. You keep me going James."

"So you just gone take the words right out of my mouth huh? So unfair."

They both laugh heartily. By the time the laughter wears off, Lauryn had pulled in to the parking space of the restaurant.

"This place brings back so many memories, huh Law?"

"Yup."

"There were a lot of good times here."

"Most definitely."

Lauryn sat silent for a moment and examined James's face.

"James, you sure you're alright. You don't look so good today."

"I was a little sluggish this morning, otherwise I'm fine."

"You're lookin' a little pale today. When was your last doctor's appointment?"

"Last week."

"Okay, I'm going to schedule you one today, I don't like the way you look today, I'm a little concerned."

"I'm fine Law."

"Will you please go to the doctor today? For me, please?"

"Alright, I'll go for you."

"Thank you, oh and I confirmed your dental appointment, it's tomorrow afternoon. I'll take you myself and bring you back."

"Okay, thank you."

"So what's been going on James? I know you're soaring with the program, you've come a really long way. I'm so proud of you, I can't express that enough."

"That really means a lot to me, thank you. And I'm doing really well, getting to exercise now."

"You're welcome."

They got their food shortly thereafter that minute conversation. As soon as James finished eating, they left so that James could immediately go see the doctor. Once he got there. Lauryn waited around to see what the doctor said. James was coming down with the flu unfortunately and Lauryn told James to immediately go straight to bed and that she'd call and check on him the next day.

"Hello?" James answered the phone with a very weak, groggy tone.

"Aaww, you sound horrible. Don't speak too much. I just wanted to give you a phone call to check on you, but I see you're not doin' so well."

"I feel horrible."

"I can tell. You keep resting, I'll have a nurse come look after you, okay?"

"Okay."

"Hope you feel better soon."

"Thank you."

"Bye."

After Lauryn hung up, she decided she was going to surprise James with a visit to lift his spirits a little.

This is the sickest that James has been in quite some time, but nothing would stop him from smiling when he saw his favorite girl.

"Hey beautiful," James said in that groggy tone but worse.

"Hey. Shh shh shh, try not to talk too much. You sounded so pitiful over the phone, I wanted to hopefully lift your spirits up a little bit by paying you a little visit."

"I always look forward to seeing you."

"You look worse than you sound. You're extra pale, you're shivering, and you have an awful sweat right now. Poor thing."

"I'll survive."

"Have you been throwing up too?"

"Yes."

"I can tell; this thing really got you huh? So much for a happy date."

"I'm sorry."

"What are you apologizing for?"

"I didn't want you to see that I was getting sick."

"Oh come on now, you knew I would."

"Yeah, but I didn't want you to worry so much."

"Of course I'm going to worry."

"Thank you for caring about me."

"I never stopped."

As Lauryn finished that statement, James slipped into sleep. Lauryn stuck around a little while, rubbed his head, and hummed a little tune that she always hummed when James was sick. It seemed almost as if James could tell it was that little tune because he immediately started to calm down little by little. After James was in a good rhythm of sleep, Lauryn left and went home.

James was sick for about a week missing his dental appointment, Lauryn rescheduled it when he got better.

The dental appointment happened exactly a week after it was originally scheduled. James was a bit nervous, but of course his superwoman reassured him that that appointment for his improvement. Lauryn stayed in the room until he succumbed to the anesthetics, and she went into the waiting area and did some work until she was called back in to see the results. Lauryn saw his new teeth before James did because James didn't come to for a little while after the surgery had ended. Lauryn loved what the dentist had done; the best part is, nobody had to pay for it. Lauryn and that dentist go back a little while and she had done something for that dentist that was actually unrepayable, she saved his life, so he promised her one huge favor, and he followed suit. Lauryn was grateful that the dentist didn't go back on his word.

A little while into a conversation that the dentist and Lauryn were having, James comes to.

"Well hey sleepy head."

"Hey there."

"How you feelin'?"

"I don't know."

"Well everything went exceptionally well and I gotta say, your teeth look great."

"May I have a mirror?"

James was handed a mirror, he looked at his teeth, and it's almost as if he went backwards in time ten years.

James broke down and cried he was so full of joy. Lauryn explain to the dentist that those were happy tears that he was crying.

After that day, James soared through the rest of that program and came out of it sober, refreshed, reeducated, and with another chance at life. Not to mention that he and Lauryn were seeing each other regularly and Lauryn even took him out on a few other "dates."

Life is great for James and it just keeps getting better. The rehab facility was so proud of James's progress and advancement that they helped him to find a job that accepted his past and his degree. This job gave James a nice salary with benefits, this salary was nice enough that James got a car and an apartment in the same building as Lauryn.

Not only was James happy with life, Lauryn was happy as well. She got her old best friend back and then some. They had actually begun a small courtship, they decided to have a date night every Saturday night since that was both of their days off.

Every now and again, James would have to cancel on Lauryn because he wasn't feeling well. Lauryn was perfectly okay with it. In fact, there were days that she would make him cancel because he struggled not to look ill, but of course Lauryn could see through any façade. As soon as she spotted James wasn't feeling well, she made him march right up stairs and get in the bed. Some days, depending on how bad a shape he was in, she would go up to his apartment with him and make sure he was okay and she would slip away when he slept.

One specific Saturday, James was feeling the absolute worst that he had felt in a very long time, but he didn't want to let Lauryn know that because it was her birthday and he didn't want to ruin her special day. Usually on dates, Lauryn would volunteer to drive and she did most of the time, but James wanted to spoil Lauryn and drive her this time.

James and Lauryn met at their usual meeting point, outside of the apartment building at the parking lot, and immediately Lauryn saw that James was in horrible condition.

"James, you look horrible. There's no way in the world I'm gonna let you leave this apartment complex."

"I'm fine Law, it's your birthday, and we're going to celebrate. I got you all dressed up, I'm dressed up, I made a reservation somewhere very nice and we are going."

James had such a determination that Lauryn couldn't fight; plus she found it rather sweet that James wanted to suffer because it was her birthday.

"So where are we going? Am I allowed to know?"

"No ma'am, you are not."

They arrived at James's car, James opened and closed the door for Lauryn and got in himself. After a bit of driving, they arrived in this beautiful restaurant that had this gorgeous stone fountain in the front of it. The building was a sandstone color with black lettering on it, the lighting was dim, and the inside had the most elegant black furniture that Lauryn had ever seen. This place was a dream come true for her.

"Oh my goodness James, this place is beautiful. How did you find it?"

"A beautiful place to celebrate a beautiful woman."

"Aaww, you know how to make a girl feel mighty special."

"I'm just trying to start my thank yous now."

"Oh stop, for what?"

"Everything. Look at me, because of you and God I'm established again. I have a great job, a nice apartment, a car. I feel like a rejuvenated me and I just want to show my superwoman some appreciation."

"You know you don't ever have to thank me James. That's what I'm here for. We're friends, friends do things for each other. If it were the other way around, I'm sure you would've done everything in your power to help me."

"You're right. I really value our friendship Law. At least take this thank you for sticking by me through all of this."

"Fine, I'll take that. It was no trouble, like I said...friends are there for each other."

As Lauryn was making these statements, she could tell that James was declining in his condition all the time.

When the food finally came to James and Lauryn he started to tremble. After the tremble turned into a full convulsion of his body, he began to foam at the mouth and he fell out of his chair on the floor still convulsing.

Lauryn was so stunned at what was happening because she had never seen James in such a bad condition before. Though she was panicking, she kept a level head and dialed 911. This is not the first time that something like this has happened in Lauryn's presence; she has had numerous clients and church members to fall to seizures or just to pass out. This time was different, this time it was someone she held close to her heart; the feeling was different, but she kept a level head nonetheless.

In less than 10 minutes, the ambulance was there, James was stabilized and on his way to the hospital. Lauryn was able to ride the ambulance with him, so she kept him calm the whole way there.

Upon arrival at the hospital, James was immediately taken to the Intensive Care Unit into a room that just seemed to have an overwhelmingly comfortable vibe. Lauryn figured that James must've been in a situation like this before.

Doctors gave James some treatments of a kind before Lauryn was allowed in the room. When Lauryn walked back in the room, James was soundly asleep.

A few hours later, James slowly opened his eyes to the least amount of sight, smiled at first, then frowned.

"Look who's awake."

"Hey beautiful," James halfway muttered.

"Poor thing, you sound so weak. Is everything alright? You scared me."

"I'm so sorry you had to see that Law, but since you've seen it, I have something of great importance to tell you."

"Of course, you know you can tell me anything."

"Well…"

Chapter 7: Speak on it, James

Is he finally going to tell me what's been going on with him? Ever since his first few stays at the hospital, I was afraid that there was something was really wrong. Lord, what could it be? Whatever it is, I know he's strong enough to get through it now...but Lord, please watch over him and keep him...

***

At first, James was very hesitant to share the news with Lauryn.

"James, you don't have to tell me right now, it's okay."

"No, it needs to be said Law."

"Alright fine, what's going on?"

James exhaled heavily and started choking back tears. "Do you remember the two times that I escaped rehab to go get high?"

"Of course."

"Well, it's because of the same reason that I fell out in a seizure at the restaurant."

"Okay James, will you please tell me what's going on?"

James took another deep breath. "The first time I ran off was because I was diagnosed with Lymphoma."

Lauryn hung her head and held James's hand.

"The second time...I ran off...was because...I found out that...it's stage four."

Oh my God. James has already been through so much Lord, but I know that Your plan is in full effect and he's going to come out with a victory.

"Oh my goodness James."

"That's not all."

"Tell me."

"Ten years ago, I left the face of the earth because my mother died...Lymphoma killed my mother."

"I remember the day you told me she died...it really broke you. I tried my best to say and do anything to calm you down and comfort you, but nothing worked; and I read about your mother's death, I thought it was a car accident."

"What you read didn't tell the whole story."

"What's the whole story?"

"That day, my mom called me and told me it was her day to go get her chemotherapy treatment. I insisted that I take her, chemo already made her weak and she wasn't exactly feeling her best that day anyway. On her way to the hospital, she had an episode and passed out at the wheel. What made it worse was that she was on the interstate and her head made the wheel spin out of control, the car flipped and she was dead before any response team came."

Lauryn exhaled deeply, "Jesus. Why didn't you tell me James? You know I would've been right there by your side through it all."

"I know you would have Law, but I personally couldn't take the news back then, and to find out that I inherited what killed my mother made me scared out of my life and I needed to get away. I wasn't thinking back then, on either occasion. Not only that, I blamed myself for the longest time thinking it was my fault for not picking her up that day…why didn't I pick her up?! I shoulda been there, Law. None of this would've ever happened had I been there that day…"

"James, you gotta know that I will always be here for you. Look at me…always. No matter what's going on, no matter the situation, whatever's going on; know that you can call on me. Now that I know all of this, I'm going to stay on top of things. If ever you forget that you have a doctor's appointment, I'll remember. You can't possibly get through this on your own, James. Will you let me be here for you?"

James broke all the way down, crying. "Will you please never leave my side?"

"I'm here James…I'm here."

James sat there crying for about a half an hour, while he was crying, Lauryn was praying. Lauryn was praying so hard that she would be strong enough for the two of them. James has seen much sorrow; now Lauryn was going to make sure that even through all these difficult times, James was going to be happy, or at least content.

After about three days, James was released from the hospital. Despite everything that went on, Lauryn did preach that Sunday, it was a rather short service since she wanted to get back to the hospital to tend to James. Upon James's discharge, Lauryn got off of work a little earlier so that she could pick James up in a reasonable amount of time. James has never been happier to see Lauryn.

"Did somebody request door-side service?"

"Hey beautiful! Such a stunning sight for aching eyes."

"How you feelin? You ready to get out of here?"

"I feel so much better now that you're here, and I'm so ready to get out of here."

"Good, let's get out of here."

Not too long after getting in the car for the ride, James noticed that it was early.

"You got off early for me?"

"I sure did. My boss said he was tired of seeing my face anyway. Little do you know, I really haven't had a day off in a very long time. I know I only got off a couple hours early, but it's a lot compared to all of this overtime I've been working as well."

"At any rate, I feel special."

Lauryn chuckled as she fastened James in and got in her vehicle herself. As soon as Lauryn got in and buckled up, in her peripheral sight, she caught a glimpse of James of staring at her.

"You alright sir?"

"No, but I know I will be."

James reached for Lauryn's hand and held it through the whole ride to the apartment building.

Luckily for James, the apartment building had an elevator so Lauryn guided the weak James to the elevator, into his room, and tucked him in.

"Alright James, I'll stay here until I know for sure you'll stay sleep then I'll go downstairs to my place."

"Okay."

"You need anything?"

"Can I trouble you for some water?"

"It's no trouble at all. Bottle or cup?"

"Bottle please."

"Straw?"

"Yes please."

"Coming right up."

"Thank you."

Lauryn hurried to get the water for James, in less than a minute, she was back in his room with a bottle of water and a straw.

"Do you need some help sitting up or you got it?"

"I would love some assistance."

"I got you."

Lauryn is actually surprisingly stronger than anybody thinks. She uses the gentlest touch to raise James up into a comfortable enough position so that he could sip the water. Lauryn sat on the side of the bed holding the water bottle as he sipped and he nodded his head when he had enough. She put the water bottle down and got James back into his comfortable place lying all the way down.

She stayed there, on the side of the bed, until James was in an unconscious sleep and went downstairs. Lauryn herself went to sleep for a few hours and went to work. Lauryn worked a full workday and was on the way home when she got a phone call from James.

"Look who's awake. You alright?"

"Yeah, I feel a little better."

"You sound a little better. I'm just getting off of work, you need anything while I'm still out?"

"No ma'am."

"Are you sure?"

"Yes ma'am, thank you though."

"Alright. How weak do you feel?"

"A little bit stronger than yesterday."

"That's good."

"I just pulled in, I'm gonna come up there for a few minutes. Is that alright with you?"

"Of course it is."

"Be up there in a minute."

"Okay."

Lauryn went upstairs to James's apartment in almost perfect timing. James was doubled over on the floor throwing up. Lauryn immediately ran to the rescue, got a trashcan, grabbed him, and comforted him until he was done. James was shaking a bit after that, but it wasn't bad. Lauryn cleaned up the floor and waited for his body to calm down for her to talk to him.

"How you feelin'?"

"I thought I was feeling better. I feel worse than I did yesterday, now."

"Where do you think that little attack came from?"

"The treatment they gave me yesterday at the hospital."

"Do you know what it was?"

"They said it was an emergency injection of my chemo regiment."

"Oh, okay. You need anything while I'm up?"

"No, but when you sit down, can I have some water?"

"You sure can."

"Thank you."

"I'm so sorry you're going through all of this James."

"Now that I know I have you, I feel better about getting through it."

"You've always had me, James."

"I know, but this is something different Law, this is life changing. What we've been through was much smaller than this, and I already know there are gonna be some difficult times."

"That's what a real friend is for James, to be here for you. I know there are gonna be rough days and long nights, but there are also gonna be great days and nights full of rest."

"You really keep my mind lifted. You have no idea how much I appreciate you, Law. You're sticking with me even through this…"

"I'm keeping to my promise, James. I told you I would always be here for you no matter what."

"You and God are the only ones that have stuck to that promise."

"Rest assured that God is always gonna do just what He said He would do. Just like He said He's gonna get you through this and you're gonna prosper."

"Really?"

"Yup, would you really question God, James?"

"Not at all."

After that statement, James drifted off into a deep sleep. Lauryn sat there and prayed for a little while then snuck downstairs to her apartment.

James would sleep uninterrupted for the remainder of the week and once he woke up, he felt brand new. He woke up midday the following Monday and decided to surprise Lauryn for lunch with lunch and a single red rose.

"Hey. What you doin' here?"

"Please tell me you haven't eaten yet."

"I haven't, what's up?"

"Just brought a little something for you."

"Well aren't you sweet. Thank you James, and the rose is beautiful."

"Only a portion as beautiful as you are."

Lauryn couldn't help but to grin in the biggest way. That made her day in ways she couldn't imagine. It was a really bad day for Lauryn, she was surpassed exhausted, another hard case came in, and she recently lost a church member she was really close to. This special delivery did so many wanders to her mood she decided to call to thank him once more after she got home from work.

"You didn't have to do that. That was really sweet of you, James."

"Oh yes I did have to do that. After everything that you've done and are doing for me, I gotta spoil you too sometimes."

"You don't ever have to spoil me, James. I'm spoiled enough."

"You always say that. You really value our friendship that much?"

"Of course, why wouldn't I?"

"I'm just simply amazed."

"You ought to be over that by now."

They both chuckled.

"How you doin' today beautiful?"

"You beat me to the punch, I was just getting ready to ask how you were feeling. But I'm good. You really made my day in ways you won't ever be able to imagine and I really appreciate you coming to see me."

"That was only a small portion of my appreciation. Oh, guess what!"

"What?"

"I'm feeling well enough to go to work tomorrow."

"That's great."

"Yeah, you know what that means?"

"What?"

"We have a date to go on, on Saturday."

"Save your money and your energy. Maybe next week, matter of fact, week after; bills are due next week."

"You're always looking out for me."

"Somebody has to."

The two agreed to end the conversation there, James told Lauryn to get some rest and Lauryn told James to get ready for work. Before James went to sleep for the night, he decided to text Lauryn and the text said: "How did I get to be so blessed? Good night Law. ☺" Lauryn went to sleep that night in the best mood she's been in in a very long time. The following morning, Lauryn decided to text James; that text said: "Good morning Mr. Willard, glad to know you're doing better. Have a productive day."

The two went to work floating on cloud nine. It seemed as though those two weeks flew by and as Lauryn promised, James took Lauryn out for their weekly date.

Lauryn let James drive, and they were going in the same direction of the restaurant they were at for Lauryn's birthday.

"James, are we going back to that place?"

"Yes ma'am. I have to make it up to you girl. Your birthday was sorta ruined because of me."

"My birthday was not ruined and you don't have to make up for anything."

"Oh yes I do, it was your birthday Law. Instead of me doing for you, you still ended up doing something for me. I gotta make up for that. You look stunning by the way."

"Thank you. You look rather handsome yourself."

"Why thank you, my best friend bought me this suit."

"She has some very good taste."

"Yes she does."

The two laughed all the way to the door of that beautiful restaurant, and it just so happened that they were seated at the very table they sat at for Lauryn's birthday.

"How convenient we're at the same table we were at for my birthday."

"I might've made a phone call."

"So you think you slick."

"Maybe a little."

That night was full of laughs and the conversation was very light. There was no mention of any negativity that evening. After eating and James paid the bill, they sat there for a moment longer because James had something of importance to ask Lauryn.

James held both of Lauryn's hands. "Law?"

"Yes? Everything alright?"

"Everything is fine, everything is great thanks to you. There's something I want to ask you, Law."

"Go for it."

All of a sudden, James got extremely nervous and was at a loss of words for a moment. "Law, you know I'm so happy you're in my life and I'm SO grateful that you've stayed with me through all of this."

"Yes, I know."

James looked down and exhaled deeply.

"Something wrong James?"

"No. Everything is right. Law, will you do me the privilege and the honor of going steady with me?"

"Oh my goodness James. The honor and the privilege is all mine."

They both got up and hugged each other so tightly they could barely draw a breath. After that, they left holding hands.

James was speechless throughout the car ride. He couldn't believe that Lauryn said yes.

"Can I share some truth with you James?"

"Sure."

"I've been waiting for you to ask me that question since the tenth grade. I knew you were this great guy: a love for God and your family, caring, a sense of humor, generous, chivalrous, polite, respectful, you present yourself very well, I could go on and on forever. I've had a crush on you for the longest time, and developing our friendship the way we have in the past and currently just made it so much better because I was okay with not being with you as long as I was still involved in your life somehow. I actually gave up on finding someone for me or that someone finding me. Tonight, you've revived my hopes that there's still some good in me."

"Can I share something with you, Law?"

"Of course."

"I've been scared out of my mind to ask you that question since the *ninth* grade. When I first laid eyes on you, I immediately noticed something different about you. You definitely weren't like the other girls. We have so much in common and appreciate each other's differences. I knew I had to be with you but the fear in me had me stuck. I wish I would've known that you actually felt the same way about me back then."

This portion of the conversation was said in the parking lot of the apartment complex. Once they finished sharing feelings, James walked Lauryn to her apartment, kissed her on the hand, and said good night.

For the next three months, it was pure bliss for the happy couple. Both of their jobs were going extremely well, James was doing so well that he was off chemotherapy for a while. Things were looking up.

Lord, You did it again. Everything is going so well.

One day, while the loving couple was relaxing at Lauryn's apartment, James began choking on what Lauryn thought was air, but was really blood. Lauryn saw the blood, got a trashcan and a towel. After he was finished, Lauryn rushed James to the hospital.

Lord, I know we can get through this. Give James the strength to see his own strength through You Lord.

Lauryn was preparing for the worst, but praying for the best. Unfortunately, the worst has occurred. The cancer came back with fierce aggression.

Chapter 8: The Storm

Lord, whatever You have in store for us I know is for the best. Through it all, we'll both praise You.

***

All of this snuck up on both James and Lauryn. James was doing so well and he wasn't feeling bad at all.

James was in ICU for four weeks and he was unconscious for two of those weeks. Lauryn spent a lot of time in the hospital with James, but she still managed to go to work and preach at church with a level head.

One day, Lauryn walked in the room and James had his eyes open.

Lauryn was sure to whisper so that James wouldn't have too much of a headache. "Hey handsome. How you feelin'?"

James's speech was a little incomprehensible, but he managed to mutter a few words. "I feel bad."

"I'm sure you do. Are you in much pain?"

"Yes."

After James responded, he slipped back into sleep and Lauryn stayed with him overnight and went to work from the hospital. It was a very long work day for Lauryn, the day went by very slowly and she was so swamped with work, by the time she was halfway done, she had worked three hours overtime. In realizing what time it was, Lauryn gathered all of the work she had left and scurried to the hospital.

When Lauryn got to James's room her heart stopped. James had gone code blue, he was no longer breathing. James was succumbing to the cancer that had so vastly usurped his body.

After a while, everybody stopped and there was one doctor still looking over James, he had two fingers on his wrist to check his pulse one final time, nothing. Just as the doctor was about to call time of death and as Lauryn was breaking down, James drew a strong uneven breath. James was indeed alive.

God, You never cease to amaze me.

As soon as James was stabilized, Lauryn was allowed into the room. She sat there on the side of his bed in shear amazement. James is not supposed to be alive, but there he was, breathing. After several hours, James managed to slightly open his eyes.

"Hey handsome. Don't say anything, okay? Save your breath and your energy."

James nodded his head.

"Oh my goodness James, you gave me the scare of my life…but I thank God you're still here. I almost lost you."

A single tear ran down Lauryn's face which made a single tear run down James's face. Lauryn got a tissue and wiped his tear away.

"Don't cry on my account sweetheart, this was a tear of joy. I'm still able to spend time with you."

James slipped into a very relaxed sleep as Lauryn was saying what she said. Once James got into a solidified sleeping pattern, Lauryn went home to get herself together and prepare for work.

As soon as Lauryn got home, she went into her room, sat at the edge of her bed, and cried hysterically for the first time in a very long time. She released the tears of the pain she felt for almost losing her significant other, she released the tears of happiness that James is still alive. Lauryn let go of so much of everything in the time she spent crying that evening. After that, she didn't know what to feel, she was exhausted so she got ready for work and went to bed.

The next day, James woke up with such energy and strength that he stunned the doctors, nurses, and even himself. Granted, James still felt very weak, but he definitely felt a hundred times better. James was under observation that whole day and was being watched around the clock, but there were no sounds of his health declining again. James's doctor kept calling Lauryn all day to keep her updated and by the end of her work day, she practically teleported to the hospital.

"Hey beautiful."

"You have no idea how good it sounds to hear your voice, no matter how weak you sound; and you have no idea how good it feels to see you breathing and moving. How are you?"

"A million times better now that you're here. How are you?"

"I feel a million times better knowing that you're still here. How you feelin'?"

"That's another story, but knowing that my baby is here, I feel better already."

Lauryn smiled, she could tell he was doing a lot better than he was the day before. On the inside, Lauryn was jumping up and down rejoicing and praising God.

After about another week, James was finally released from the hospital. James was gaining his strength back slowly, but he was still restricted to bed rest for at least two weeks. During that time, Lauryn made sure she got off of work on time every day so that she could hurry home and tend to James.

James tried not to seem needy, but he needed a lot of attention. Lauryn didn't mind giving it to him; after all, they are together.

"Hey beautiful, sit down for a minute."

"What's up?"

"Nothing, I just wanted you to take a minute to rest yourself. You're running around trying to take care of me and do all of your work. You just need a minute."

"Well thank you for being so considerate, but I'm cleaning the bathroom. It hasn't been cleaned in a while and I don't want you to get sick all over again. Have you started to gain an appetite yet or no?"

"No, not really."

"Okay. You need anything right now?"

"No ma'am, I'm fine at the moment. Thank you."

"Alright, let me know if you need something."

"You're so good to me."

Lauryn looked at James, smiled, kissed him on the cheek, and went back to cleaning the bathroom.

After Lauryn finished cleaning the bathroom, she peeped into James's room and saw that he had fallen asleep and was sleeping rather peacefully.

James slept until the next day. When he woke up, he mustered up the strength to call Lauryn during her lunch hour.

"Hey Mr. Willard. How are you?"

"I'm quite alright, how are you?"

"I'm fine. How you feelin'?"

"Better."

"That's good, you sound a little stronger."

"Yeah, I figured if I could pick up the phone by myself, then I'm feeling a bit better."

"I'm happy for you. You sound well rested."

"I had a good amount of sleep."

"You sure did."

"Well, I just wanted to call you and let you know that I am yet alive darlin'."

"Good to know."

"Bye beautiful."

"See you later."

After they each hung up, Lauryn went back to work until it was time for her to get off. It was a moderate work day for Lauryn; she got by without working any over time.

When Lauryn got to James's apartment, she saw that he was sitting up on his own.

"Look at you, Superman, sittin' up and stuff."

They both laughed.

"Just thought I'd show you my new trick of the day."

"Well I like," Lauryn applauded what was actually a big feat for James.

Lauryn did a couple things around James's apartment and when she caught a glimpse of James, he was staring at her.

"What you eyein' me for?"

"Just basking in all of your beauty, that's all."

"Haha, bask away I guess."

James continued to look at Lauryn.

"Okay James, what's really going on sweetheart?"

"I'm just trying to figure out how I got such a wonderful, blessed, intelligent, caring, beautiful, lovely, did I mention beautiful, woman like yourself."

"I don't know, I guess you're gonna have to ask God to find out."

"How about I thank Him instead?"

"Sounds like a plan."

"And you're so good to me. You treat me like a king, you spoil me."

"Are you hungry?"

"See, just like that."

"Are you gonna answer the question?"

"I am hungry a little bit."

"Alright, I figured since you're getting a little bit of your strength back and you're past your bed rest time, we'd go grab something just to get you some fresh air."

"Stop reading my mind girl. I've been wanting to get out of this place for a little while."

"You wanna keep being Superman and let me help you walk, or do you want me to grab the wheelchair?"

"All of the above."

"Smart man. Wait right here, I'll load up my truck and we'll get out of here."

"Yes ma'am."

Lauryn put James's wheelchair in her trunk and went back upstairs to go get James. To Lauryn's wonderful surprise, James was standing up near his bed patiently waiting for her.

"Well look at you, two tricks in one day? This calls for celebration. You ready to hit it?"

"Get me out of here."

James did surprisingly well down the stairs; James wanted to go down the stairs just to see how well he could use his legs.

"I'm proud of you Mr. Willard."

"Thank you, love."

James lost a bit of strength and was drained once he got to the vehicle. Lauryn buckled him up and got in herself.

They didn't go too far past the apartment complex, but James wanted to try his hand at walking again so he insisted that they go in and order. He mustered up some strength and walked in almost as easily as he walked down the stairs.

The couple ordered some food to go and James walked out of the restaurant with almost no assistance from Lauryn. Lauryn was so pleased with James's almost instantaneous progress, she couldn't do anything but smile at James.

"What you smilin' at girl?"

"You. How far you've come. I'm so proud of you James, you haven't given up and you're moving forward. And I'm so happy that you're working toward getting back to you."

"Thank you, baby. I'm happy with how well my body is healing. Prayer is doing so many wonders for me. God is so awesome."

"Yes, He is."

By the time the couple got back to their apartment building, James was completely drained. Lauryn put him in the wheelchair to get him to the elevator and into his apartment. Since James was so drained and weak, Lauryn fed him his dinner. James ate a good portion of his food before he was full. The night was a little rough for James, so Lauryn stuck around all night. By morning, James finally fell into a deep, sound sleep.

Lauryn was so hoping that James was going to be sleep when she got off of work, he had such a rough night so he needed his sleep. When Lauryn got to James's apartment, she carefully opened the door to peep in before she walked in; James was sound asleep.

James didn't hear anything that Lauryn was doing, she wrote a note to let him know that she was off of work and to call her when he woke up.

After Lauryn placed the note on James's nightstand, she gently kissed him on the forehead and went downstairs to her apartment.

Shortly after Lauryn left James's apartment, James woke up, saw the note and called Lauryn.

"Good evening Mr. Willard how are you?"

"I'm fine. How are you?"

"I'm fine. How you feelin'?"

"A little stronger and a little better."

"That's good. Do you need anything?"

"I don't wanna trouble you, baby."

"You know it's not any trouble, what you need?"

"My throat is really dry and the water by my nightstand is gone and I'm starting to get a little hungry."

"I'll be right up there."

"Don't waste your energy, I'll survive."

"No sweetheart, if there's something you need, then I'm gonna make sure you have it. I know you're not feeling well and that leaves your body weak. I'll be up there in less than five minutes."

"Ya know, next to God and my mother, you're the best thing that's ever happened to me."

"Sure, sure. I'm coming up the stairs now."

"I'm serious girl."

"I know you are, and here I come."

Lauryn hung up the phone and walked through the door. James happily greeted her by mustering up the strength to sit up, hug, and kiss her.

Once Lauryn did everything that James requested, she decided to sit and chat with him for a little while.

"So what's going on Mr. Willard?"

"Nothing really. I've just been thinking about the bills this month."

"I figured you were gonna say something along those lines. But you don't have to worry about that, you know why?"

"Why?"

"Back when you were still in rehab on the way out, I started you a rainy day savings account. And when you got your job, I just so happened to tell them to put a portion in this account just in case you couldn't work for a while."

"Lauryn Nevaeh Jones, you are something else, you know that? How did you think of that without knowing that I was sick?"

"I mean, I figured something wasn't right, plus you never know, sick or not, when you won't be able to work."

"Mm, beautiful and smart too."

"Oh stop."

"Where are your flaws woman?!"

"Everywhere, you're just choosing not to acknowledge them."

"Super smart. But somebody gotta compliment you without putting you down."

"That's why you're mine, you keep me going James."

"You look exhausted Law."

"You know, you tell me that at least once a week." Lauryn chuckled.

"Because you look exhausted every day."

"I get my sleep."

"Do you?"

"Yes I do, I get an appropriate amount."

"What do you call an appropriate amount?"

"Enough, that's what I call an appropriate amount. What you so worried about me for?"

"Because you look so tired love, I can't help but to be concerned."

"Well you don't have time to be worried about me. You need to worried about you and getting better, that's all you need to worry about right now. When you fully recover, we'll see."

"You think I'm gonna fully recover?"

"Of course. Why do you doubt it?"

"Every time I get better and things are going well, I get knocked down by this sickness."

"You're gonna come out of this James. You're gonna recover, and you're gonna go into remission. I know it, I feel it. You just gotta believe in yourself enough and have the faith in God that He's gonna heal you."

"Every time I knock myself down you pick me back up. I have one request for you ma'am."

"What can I do for you sir?"

"Go to bed."

"Nope, sorry, can't do that."

"And why not?"

"It's third Wednesday baby, I gotta go teach Bible study."

"What would your members do without you?"

"Join another church."

"Funny, you should be a Christian comedienne."

"Haha, you're chock full of jokes yourself."

"What time is Bible study?"

"In about an hour."

"You already have your lesson prepared?"

"Yes sir."

"How far in advance do you prepare?"

"When the spirit hits."

"Ah."

James and Lauryn sat staring each other for about a minute.

"I don't understand why you gotta keep lookin' at me like that sir."

"Because at every gaze, I find something more beautiful about you, inside and out."

"Well you're a regular ole Shakespeare aren't you? With your so-called smooth ways and your nickel slick talk."

"I try."

They both laugh. After a moment of silence, Lauryn gets ready to get up and go back downstairs so she can change clothes and go church.

"Alright Mr. Willard, I'm going to let you rest and I'm going to go downstairs to change and get ready for church. You have a good evening, I'll call you later."

"Yes ma'am."

After that, they shared a goodbye kiss and Lauryn left.

Lauryn was indeed exhausted, so she kept her lesson rather short. It seemed almost as if her members felt the same way she did, as soon as he walked into the room, everybody looked exhausted. To keep the mood vibrant, she filled the room with laughter. Bible study ended within an hour and Lauryn was headed back home.

Upon getting in her SUV, Lauryn called James.

"Good evening."

"Hello Mr. Willard. How are you?"

"I'm peachy, how are you?"

"I'm fine. You need anything before I make my way back home?"

"No, but when you get back, can you come back to my place?"

"I sure can."

"Thank you ma'am."

"You're welcome, sir."

James had something of great importance that he wanted to share with her. Lauryn drove home and wondered what is was that James wanted Lauryn to come back over.

"Hey handsome."

"Hello lovely. Have a seat please madam."

"Alright. What's going on?"

"First of all, happy six months baby."

"You remembered?!"

Lauryn was stunned and rather taken aback by James's knowledge of the date that they got together. Of course Lauryn remembered, but that day was running together with the rest of the days, she never really took the time to look at the calendar to see what the date was.

"Of course I remembered. The day that I got to entitled to my best friend as my girlfriend was the second happiest day of my life."

"The second? What was the first?"

"Meeting you."

"Aaww, you silver tongued fox you. You're so sweet."

"I'm just telling the truth. My life is a million times better with you…I love you Lauryn…I'm in love with you."

Lauryn was at a complete loss for words. She was completely stunned; James professed his love for Lauryn. Lauryn quickly gathered her thoughts.

"You know, it's kinda funny, I've dreamt of the day you would say that to me. I've dreamt of my reaction, but it wasn't this. In my imagination, I would say it, but not with as much feeling that I have now. I love you too James, so much more than you know."

The two shed a single tear simultaneously and hugged each other with such passion that they didn't even notice the time that went by.

When they let each other go, they just stared at each other.

"I love you, Lauryn."

"I love you, too."

Lauryn looked at the clock on the nightstand and realized how late it was, kissed James good night, and went downstairs to prepare for the next day.

For James, it was almost as if "I love you" were the three magic words. After that day, James just kept getting better and better, stronger and stronger.

Lauryn noticed the miraculous improvements that James was making and couldn't do anything but smile at him and praise God all the time.

Thank You Lord! You keep doing things in such in such amazing ways! Thank You for continuing to bless us.

Within a week, James was back on his feet and back to work. This is the best that James has ever felt. He felt liberated, he was blissfully happy, he was well. James was in a state of euphoria, he reached his Omelas.

It's Saturday, it's date night. James was in such a good mood, before date night began, he filled up both his car and Lauryn's. For this particular date night, James told Lauryn to stay in her apartment, he was gonna come down there, cook for her and wait on her hand and foot. At first Lauryn didn't like the idea of being waited on hand and foot, but the idea grew on her.

The time came for date night to commence, and James was right on time.

"Good evening my queen."

James was dressed in this elegant black fitted tuxedo with a crisp white shirt that had black buttons and he had a nice slim bowtie on; along with that, he had on these exquisite black cufflinks. His shoes were so shiny one would think that they were spit-shined and polished by the military.

"Come on in sir."

James walked in and pulled from behind him this beautiful bouquet of red roses, the red was so deep and rich Lauryn thought that the flowers were fake, but they were indeed real.

"Now that I'm in here, you go sit down and you won't lift a finger for the remainder of the evening."

Lauryn still didn't know how she felt about being waited on hand and foot by James; she didn't want him to do too much and he go backwards.

"Sounds like a plan, but before I sit down, do you need any help with anything?"

"No. Now go sit down."

"Yes sir."

James brought a movie over, it was a movie that Lauryn hadn't had the chance to see in the theater and it was just released on DVD. As Lauryn was sitting down, James was setting up the movie. Lauryn was sitting up at the time, and after James set up the movie, he moved her legs so that they were stretched on the couch, he placed a good pillow behind her back, and he placed a cover on top of her.

Lauryn has never been this comfortable, she was watching a great movie, her other half was cooking for her, and she was completely relaxed. This was the perfect night so far.

As James was cooking, he let Lauryn sample everything and Lauryn was falling in love more and more with every bite. James cooked this wonderful chicken that was so tender it practically melted in her mouth, it was seasoned to perfection. For the sides, James prepared some fresh green beans that he snapped the night before and mashed potatoes from scratch. They washed it all down with an appropriately aged merlot. What made the meal more perfect was it was brought to her and James fed every single bite to her.

"Did you enjoy the meal?"

Lauryn couldn't do anything but shake her head at the moment and James laughed.

"Was it that good?"

"Most definitely. Oh my goodness James, I did not know you could throw down like that."

"I have a couple hidden talents."

"That meal was amazing James, and that wine…wow."

"I'm ever so glad you're enjoying your evening."

"You really know how to spoil a sistah."

"Just trying to do a portion of the spoiling you do to me. But the evening is not over yet ma'am."

"What could possibly be next?"

James smiled mischievously, turned the TV off, and turned the music on. James knew that when Lauryn unwinds, she listens to soothing music, so he turned that soothing music up, took Lauryn by the hand and they danced all around the apartment.

Lauryn was having the night of her life and she didn't want it to end. She felt so secure in her man's arms and he smelled so good. Every now and again, they would look into each other's eyes and Lauryn noticed a certain twinkle the James had in his eyes and they couldn't do anything but smile at each other when they were looking at each other.

This night was absolute perfection for Lauryn.

It was starting to get late, and James knew that Lauryn had to get up early for church as did he. James literally swept Lauryn off her feet, unraveled the covers, placed her in the bed, tucked her in, said a short prayer, and kissed her good night.

James went in the kitchen, washed the dishes, straightened up the place, and left to go to bed himself. James knew that Lauryn was sleep, so he decided to send a nice long text for her to wake up to. The text read: "Hey there beautiful, I just wanted to let you know that I love you so much and there is not a day that goes by that I don't thank God for you. God made you just for me, and I thank you for being you at all times. I am so far beyond blessed that you're in my life that it brings me to tears every time just thinking of the notion that you're real. You are too good to be true. I don't deserve you. I love you my sweet perfection."

The next morning, Lauryn's cell phone alarm went off as usual, and she saw the text message. Immediately, Lauryn's face started glowing. She decided to wait and see James's face to thank him for such a beautiful message.

Lauryn got dressed, grabbed her Bible and headed out the door; James was waiting for her by her vehicle.

"Oh my goodness James, that was such a loving message to wake up to. Thank you."

"Just showing my appreciation for you, my love."

"Well I appreciate your appreciation."

"Please allow me to drive you to church this morning and later after service."

"Permission granted."

James opened Lauryn's door, closed it once she was in comfortably, and got in himself.

They rode in blissful silence all the way to the church, and once again, James opened Lauryn's door. Once he opened the door, James held his hand out to help Lauryn get out of the truck. They held hands walking to Lauryn's office, and Lauryn never touched a door, nor her chair in her office.

James left the office so that Lauryn could mentally prepare for service, and he went to sit in his favorite spot.

Lauryn preached a beautiful sermon on God's timing. Yet again, God's timing was on time; a visitor accepted Jesus Christ and wanted to become a member. Lauryn left the service so full that she had to sit in her office for a while to soak everything in.

Lord, You are awesome.

Four more euphoric months passed by and before they knew it, James and Lauryn were celebrating one year of being together.

James decided to take Lauryn to that restaurant where they celebrated her last birthday. James also made sure to tell Lauryn to dress extra special because it was an extra special night, more than Lauryn knew.

James drove to the restaurant and Lauryn never touched a door nor a chair. Both Lauryn and James ordered what they had the last time and it was as exquisite as the last time, if not, a little better. As their plates were being taken away and James was giving the waiter a card for the check, he just gazed at Lauryn.

"You are so beautiful."

"You tell me that a lot."

"Because you have to be constantly reminded of your pure beauty."

"Sure, sure. You look like you have something on your mind, something wrong?"

"No ma'am, everything is just right."

James proceeded to motion his hand toward Lauryn so that she would stand up. As Lauryn stood up, James was holding Lauryn's left hand and kneeling down on one knee. As James was getting down on that knee, he began to shed tears.

"Lauryn Nevaeh Jones… I love you so much, my heart aches if I don't hear from you after so many hours. Every time something pops up in my mind that reminds me of you, I smile so hard for so long my cheeks hurt. I love you so much, I talk God's ears off thanking Him for you and praying that you stay sane through everything that you're going through with me and other facets of your life. I love you so much I cry happy tears just thinking about knowing that you're mine. Law, I can't stand the fact that I can't wake up next to you every day or hold you close next to me every night. Will you do me the absolute greatest honor and privilege of being my wife?"

As James pulled out this beautifully cut three-carat diamond, Lauryn broke down and said: "The honor and privilege is all mine. Of course I will marry you James Willard! I love you so much."

Chapter 9: Eternal Happiness

Oh my goodness! Is this really happening?! Am I really engaged? I haven't been this happy in such a long time, I forgot what happy was. I'm soon going to enjoy eternal happiness with my best friend and the love of my life.

***

"SHE SAID YES Y'ALL!!!!!!!!!!!!!!!!!!!!!!!!!!!!!!!!!"

James picked Lauryn up and spun her around numerous times. The other people in the restaurant including the staff all applauded for the newly engaged couple.

Shortly after much celebration, the happy couple left and went home. The two were so elated that they couldn't separate to go to bed. James went into Lauryn's apartment, sat on the couch and awaited Lauryn to change clothes and come back to the living room. In that time together, they simply enjoyed each other's company. They sat in complete silence, gazing at each other both with grins out of this world.

That following Monday, Lauryn went to work with a different kind of glow and it was on her left hand ring finger. All of Lauryn's subordinates and colleagues asked Lauryn about the ring. All Lauryn had to say was: "He proposed." As soon as Lauryn said that, everybody she told stopped in their tracks with their jaws dropped all the way to the floor.

The wedding was to be planned for exactly a year after the proposal. So far, everything was going according to plan. One night, while the couple was having dinner, children popped into the conversation.

"So tell me Law, do you want kids?"

"I sure do as a matter of fact. Do you?"

"Yes, I do. How many kids do you want?"

"Two. How many do you want?"

"Two."

They both laughed.

"I want a boy and a girl James."

"Will you stop stealing the thoughts out of my head woman?!"

"You really want a boy and a girl?"

"Yes. A girl to be just like her mother, and boy so that I can start a fresh legacy of doing something right."

"But you've done at least one thing right."

"And what was that? Enlighten me."

"You asked me to marry you."

"Definitely can't argue with you there."

"But back to kids, I think we should both get checked out to make sure that everything is okay."

"I am in acquiescence with you there darlin'."

They both scheduled separate appointments and one joint appointment. The joint appointment came first.

At this joint appointment, everything that was told to them was everything that they didn't want to hear. The doctor strongly advised the couple not to procreate because of James's old habits mainly and the risk factor for the child to develop Lymphoma in the terminal stage immediately was enormous. The couple wasn't having it, they both had unshakable faith in God that these children were going to be healthy, they went against that doctor's orders and proceeded with their individual appointments.

Time was growing closer and closer for the wedding and the couple was getting happier and happier. James was doing so well, he officially went into remission and was pronounced cancer free. As Lauryn was getting every little detail of her side of the wedding completed, James was doing the same. As Lauryn was picking her bridal party, James was picking his groomsmen.

The most beautiful characteristic of Lauryn and James's relationship was that they never stopped dating. Through the engagement, they still had their weekly date. Along with that, they never stopped getting to know each other. As a matter of fact, it was a part of their everyday conversations.

It's a week before the wedding, James has started to move some of his things to Lauryn's apartment because his lease was ending before the wedding and the couple closed on a house that was centrally located between Lauryn's church, Lauryn's job, and James's job. Excitement grew with every waking moment.

The day of the wedding has arrived and both Lauryn and James are so nervous. They were both filled with doubts. Would they keep each other happy? Will they forever live up to each other's expectations? Will they get tired of each other? What if they begin to dislike each other? What if something really happens to the kids like the doctor said? All of these things were on both of their minds, but as soon as the wedding commenced, they both washed away all negative thoughts.

Lauryn's bridal party had on these beautiful deep peach colored dresses; Lauryn had on this gorgeous white gown, which went all the way down and had a small train, with a white lily bouquet. Lauryn's dress was very simplistic as the bridal party's dress. The bridal party carried tiger lilies as their bouquets which were very fitting for the dresses. Lauryn got all the way down the aisle to James and James had the biggest, brightest, whitest grin he's ever had.

The ceremony was straight forward, the reverend went through his protocol, they did unity sand, and it came down to exchanging vows...

"Lauryn, because of you...I have totally transformed. I've become a better man. When we first met, I knew I had to have you, you were different from the others. God knew even back then what I didn't, you make me better. Because of you, I've overcome a longtime addiction to one of the strongest drugs out there, I've recommitted my life to Christ, I got myself together, and best of all, I got you. Thank you for being you, I'm forever indebted to you. I owe you the world, but your humble nature accepts my heart. I love you with everything in my being Lauryn. I can't wait to start my eternity with you."

"James, because of you...I know what being a blessing means. You gave me a hope that with all the love I give out, I can still give out more and you revived my hope that I could be loved. Thank you for being you. Thank you for allowing me to be me completely and wholeheartedly. I love you so much, infinity can't even describe it. I thank God for you James, because of you, I know that I will always have somebody loving me too."

After vows were exchanged, rings were put on and they said their "I do's" and the two became one. It was official, Lauryn has become Mrs. James Willard.

The two were happily married for three years before they decided to procreate. As prayed for, Lauryn had two beautiful children two years apart. Their names are James Willard, II and Erykah Faith Willard.

One Sunday, Lauryn preached on family and it was what she thought her greatest sermon. Usually, she had one of her associate ministers to do a final prayer before she did the benediction, but Lauryn decided to pray this morning.

"O Lord how excellent is thy name. God, we thank You. There have been so many storms weathered, so many wars fought, and so many wounds because of war. Thank You for staying by each and every one of our sides and defeating every demon that has crossed our paths and thank You for blessing us all along the way. Lord, we are all so undeserving of all the good that You do, yet you continue to bless us at every waking moment. Watch over us all as we continue to live for You. And the people of God said…Amen."

Amen.

Made in the USA
Columbia, SC
13 July 2018